Jingle
BEAR

INTERNATIONAL BESTSELLING AUTHOR
TK LAWYER

DEDICATION

FOR MY HUSBAND, JIM- MY OWN JINGLE
BEAR. I LOVE YOU

CHAPTER 1

ARABELLE

Brown-colored eyes as warm and as inviting as fudge, chocolate brownies, nestled, temptingly, atop a wire cooling rack, captured hers. Gabe's musical-toned laughter followed a quip posed by one of the men huddled in their small group at the local coffee house. He scratched his soft, bearded chin before he glanced at her again. His eyes shifted from her to the large turkey decoration hanging overhead. Then finally, to the man whose comical jokes wiggled and shook several of their friend's bellies, causing their mouths to open and roar with contagious laughter. Gabe widened his eyes and then shifted his gaze, again, toward the entertaining male, indicating his approval of him. Yet, Arabelle wasn't interested. No man intrigued her anymore, not after Clyde.

Gabe's date, Marnie, huddled closer

to him, possessively grabbing ahold of his arm and resting her head on it with a flirty smile. She couldn't fault Marnie for claiming what she wanted. Gabe was a good guy and truly a catch. He was also Arabelle's best friend. Although, it hadn't always been that way...

The first time they met, in third grade, he pulled her pigtails and chased her across the playground. It was only years later that she realized he liked her- as a friend. For boys, expressing emotions resulted in curious, often questionable actions. Boys teased, almost flirted, yet they also name called. They could be quite frustrating.

In ninth grade, at a high school football game, Arabelle took a giant leap and confessed her feelings for Gabe. She stood, stunned as he laughed at her. Watching Gabe's response hit her straight in the gut. For the first time in her life, she was lost, weakened, and weary like she'd been run through by an eighteen-wheeler. She swallowed down her pride, urging her to lash back at him, and, instead, calmly withdrew her comment. That day, she vowed to keep her innermost feelings a secret. She stamped down the bleachers faster than she ever had. Her cheeks burned from the effort of sharing with Gabe all she wanted for them, as well as from the disgrace.

She swept past the parking lot before she allowed herself the chance to cry. There was no way in hell she'd humiliate herself in front of him, ever again.

Since then, Gabe and Arabelle have remained best friends. She still loved him, though not in the way he might've preferred. Gabe never apologized for his harsh criticism, and Arabelle never brought it up again. She preferred to bury the disappointing outcome as far down into her gut as possible.

Gabe was now dating Marnie, a svelte, blue-eyed, tall blonde with long, lush hair and an unnatural set of full lips that likely had been plumped up in a doctor's office somewhere. Marnie was the total opposite of Arabelle, a plump, curvy girl with long, dark brown hair, brown eyes, and an all-natural set of lips Mother Nature gave her. In fact, everything on Arabelle's body was original. She doubted Marnie could state the same.

Gabe turned toward Marnie and planted a generous smooch across her lips. What was it like to kiss him? Since he held no interest in her- at least in the same way he did Marnie- she figured she'd never know. Still, tawdry images of Gabe making out with Arabelle intruded. Some scenarios she cringed at while others intrigued her. She closed her eyes and sighed out her disappointment. It would never happen. It wasn't worth thinking about.

Instead, she looked over at the man Gabe urged her to consider. Dean worked with Gabe, and they'd become recent friends. He was a decent-looking man with short, medium brown hair, bushy eyebrows, and a mustache. Compared to Dean, Gabe was rugged-looking and smoldering hot-sexy. Just one quick glance into his warm, kind eyes brought women to their knees. Well, maybe not all women... Arabelle always remained standing, yet a part of her melted every time Gabe fixed his cozy, comfortable irises on her.

Still, when females caught a glimpse of his neatly trimmed mustache and beard, they swooned in one way or the other. And if that didn't get them, his long eyelashes sweeping across his soft, impeccable skin would.

Yes. Arabelle spent way too much time observing Gabe, committing to memory all of his outstanding features while blending in like a wallflower at a nightclub. But then... Gabe was no ordinary man.

He rescued her when Clyde tore her heart out. After finding Clyde in her bedroom with her roommate, Arabelle took off for Gabe's cabin. Thankfully, he was home. Even better, he was alone.

He took her into his arms. Then he moved her into his log cabin for four months after helping her clear out her stuff from the apartment. Having co-signed a lease, the roommate demanded the rest of the money owed to her. Arabelle stared, stunned at the woman who betrayed her, holding her hand out in front of her, demanding restitution. She protested when Gabe wrote the roommate a check. Arabelle swore she'd pay him back every cent. That was a year ago. Yet, Gabe didn't care. He didn't want the money back. He wanted Arabelle to be happy.

She shook her head as the memories flowed through her. She was going to pay Gabe back every cent, even if it ended up the last thing she did. She owed him, at least that much. He was kind to her at a difficult time, taking her in when she had no other place to stay. Yet, the four months she spent in his cabin proved to be the longest months ever. Watching Gabe parade around shirtless and in his boxers was delicious yet torturous eye candy her battered heart could've done without. Still, she relished those long nights, on his sofa, when his dreamy broad shoulders cradled her from behind. With his long arms folded across her chest, they stayed cozily cuddled as they watched TV... How in the world did she ever survive the temptation he posed?

For Gabe, the months must've flown by. When he wasn't spending time with her, he was mostly at his girlfriend's house. It was a sweet effort, on his part, to give Arabelle some privacy. Yet, there was that one time his girlfriend came over.

She'd met the Spanish starlet with the perfect abs and low-cut V-neck t-shirts before, though she couldn't really say she knew her well. However, after that single night, she could tell for sure she knew her much, much better. At least in one aspect. At the very least, Arabelle now knew the precise elevation in decibels that the girl's voice rose each time Gabe pleasured her. It was possibly the longest night Arabelle spent at Gabe's place...

Gabriel Allan Caddel. That was his name. Yet everyone she knew called him Gabe. The only time she ever called him by his full first name was when she was upset with him. Unlike Gabe, she didn't have a nickname. When they were younger, Gabe teased her and called her Belly. She hated that nickname. Why couldn't he call her Belle like the female protagonist in Beauty and the Beast she loved so much? Yet, he never called her that.

Holding onto Marnie's hand, Gabe lifted from his chair, dragging her up next to him. He nodded once at Arabelle before addressing the group.

"We're going to go. Enjoy the rest of the night."

Dean piped up. He smirked as he spoke. "We know *you* will."

Gabe laughed. "Ass wipe." He pulled Marnie toward him and led her out the door.

Arabelle settled back into her chair when Dean leaned toward her. "So, you going too?"

"No. I figure I'll stay another hour."

"Let me buy you a drink, then."

"Okay." She requested a cold beer, enjoying the taste of something refreshing and slippery sliding down her throat after a long night of laughter and conversation. When the waiter dropped her bottle in front of her, she took a long swig and then closed her eyes and sighed. She gently placed the frosted glass back onto the awaiting coaster atop the long wooden table. It had been a long night, and she was a bit tired. Still, she aimed to enjoy the rest of the remaining hours without Gabe looming over her or making her decisions for her about who she should date. He always set her up when he had the chance. Yet, when she went out with the men Gabe vouched for, he became, strangely, disgruntled. Would he do the same with Dean?

"Hey, you wanna come back to my place?"

Dean lifted a quizzical eyebrow while she silently chastised herself for her hasty words. What in the hell was she thinking of? Inviting him back to her apartment. Although living in the small town of Cleveland, Tennessee didn't warrant a lot of crime. Still, some small towns were known for crazy out-of-place murders occurring. It was always the quiet ones, they said. Those were the ones to watch out for. Was Dean one of them?

Yet Dean was at a bar, drinking and cracking jokes. He couldn't be that shy, outcast personality they talked about on T.V. You know- the crazies that went home to a hidden, out of the way, collection of hatchets and knives in their workshop, right? Not that she wanted things to change, but hardly anything exciting happened in Cleveland. Still, she wasn't the kind of woman to welcome strangers home. Was she nuts? She hardly knew the man. Of course, Gabe didn't live too far from her. If she needed his intervention, she knew he'd be there to help her. Especially if she'd fallen way off her rocker on this one.

Arabelle prepared for Dean's hasty

yes while attempting to form a sound rebuttal. She formulated valid excuses in her mind, mixed in an apology. She opened her mouth to deliver her statement when he said, "No."

Snapping her mouth shut, she lifted her eyebrows in surprise at his rejection. No man ever refused such an invitation- at least, not in her experience. She was sure her best friend and long-time womanizer, Gabe, wouldn't either, given the opportunity with a willing female. Was Dean different?

"Not yet, that is. We don't know each other, and it's late. Plus, you've had a few beers, and I don't take advantage of women. Not unless they're sober and, of course, willing."

She smiled at his explanation. Dean had a sense of humor, too.

"However, I will take a rain check- that is- after we go out a few times if you're still willing. What do you say we go out first, to...dinner? Can I take you out tomorrow night?"

She blinked her eyes. Was he for real? Yet, the sincerity pooling in his eyes urged her to give him a chance.

"Sure. Why not? I'd love to go to dinner with you."

"Great. I'll pick you up at eight then? Gabe already shared with me where you live."

Her eyebrows shot up. Gabe was giving strangers her address. What in the hell? She had some choice words to say to him the next time they spoke.

"Okay. I'll see you then." She lifted up from the chair and pulled her wallet out of her purse. Dean swung his arm out in front of her, shaking his hand side to side while he said, "No. I got you."

"But it's not a date."

"Call it a pre-cursor. A little taste of what's to come."

Dean was definitely un-like the men she dated in her past.

"Well, thank you, though you don't have to do this. Still, I do appreciate it. Have a really nice night. I'll see you tomorrow."

She gave him a sweet smile as she snatched her keys. Slinging her purse over her shoulder, she strode through the front door of the establishment into the near-empty parking lot to her awaiting black SUV. Except for the bright blue pinstripes decorating each side, the basic color of the vehicle was almost invisible amidst the surrounding darkness.

Despite the standard color, she loved her car. To lose her prized possession, in any way- through theft, a car accident resulting in a total loss or- No... She didn't want to imagine it. She'd wind up a total mess if any of that occurred. She'd owned the sturdy, reliable means of transportation for almost twelve years. She was hesitant to let it go even at the prospect of a shiny, newer, fancier model. Besides, she hated car payments.

Back at her apartment, she opened the front door to tongues lolling, tails wagging, and two sets of eyes focused on her. She shoved the door closed behind her to keep her furballs from escaping.

Hunkering down in front of them, she grabbed at their faces, welcoming their random tongue licks across her hands. "Hey, you two. Have you been good?"

Junebug, her Yorkie, and Whiptail, her Lhasa Apso mix, twisted their heads up and looked at her.

"Silly girls," she said, brushing a hand over each ones' head before she sauntered over to her favorite chair and sighed happily into the cushions.

"Girls, you'd never guess the night I had."

Her furry friends crept closer. Junebug rubbed her side against Arabelle's leg and whimpered. Whiptail barked and then twirled on the rug until she found the exact right spot. She lay down, curling herself into a tight ball for warmth.

Arabelle tugged down the blanket draped over the back of the chair. She whipped the soft acrylic throw across her with a satisfied smile.

"This is so much nicer."

She had just lifted her legs onto a nearby ottoman when her doorbell sounded, proceeded by several loud knocks.

The dogs yipped and barked while running to the door. Arabelle gently pushed them aside with her legs while she viewed the visitor through the door's peephole.

"Oh. It's Gabe." She pulled on the door knob and ushered him in. "Hey. What are you doing here so late? I thought you were out with Marnie?"

Gabe gave her a disgruntled look. "I was until she threw up in my car."

After locking the door behind them, she followed him into the living room. "Oh no. Is she okay?"

He stretched his arms across the back of the couch and settled into the cushions. "Yeah, I took her home. She was feeling better by then, but I figured it was best to leave and let her rest. She thought so, too."

Possible images of the current state of Gabe's interior flashed through her mind. Arabelle grimaced while Gabe gave the dogs attention. "How is your car?"

Enthusiastically seeking his attention, Junebug and Whiptail received more pats and caresses than Arabelle figured Gabe's date got tonight. She smirked at her observation.

He answered her without taking his eyes off the dogs. "It's better now. Although I had to do a lot of cleaning and spray a ton of air freshener."

"Oh geez and on leather, too. I can imagine the work you had to do."

"Actually, if she had to throw up, I'd rather it be on leather. Easier to clean though it does get into the nooks and cracks."

She threw her hands up in the air and made a gagging sound. "Augh, enough. You're making me sick, now."

"Well, the good thing is you're already home."

She rolled her eyes and wrinkled her nose at him. "Ha-ha. Funny man. So, why are you here?"

He stretched his legs out in front of him, resting them across part of the wide, bohemian-colored ottoman, leaving the other half, vacant, for her. "I had to find out about Dean. Did you get a date with him?" His feet rested on their sides, opening his thighs wider for comfort.

She stared at the empty space between his strong thighs as tawdry images of what she could do within that small, confined, heated space entered her mind. Gabe was a devilishly handsome man.... "Actually, I did."

He patted his lap and invited her to join him. Moving over him, she sat down upon his legs, still surprised that his thick, muscled thighs could easily take her weight. Still, she lifted herself a bit off him-putting the majority of her weight on her feet-to keep from causing him discomfort until he locked gazes with her and shook his head. Apparently, he knew what she was up to. He smiled again when she relaxed into him and held her tightly within his arms.

Arabelle knew their relationship didn't quite fit the picture of what best friends should look like. Still, they remained, only best friends. In her opinion, some of the acts they engaged in seemed more like boyfriend material. He never went down that route with her, though. Yet, holding her in his lap for hours on end was likely not a definition found in any traditional dictionary's listing for "best friends."

If he was on a date right now, she'd never agree to be held within his arms, sitting on his lap, in front of his date. Yet, knowing Gabe, he might've requested this from her, anyway. As strange as their relationship sometimes seemed, she'd never let go of him, no matter what. She loved him and enjoyed having him in her life. So, if Gabe wanted her to sit on his lap forever, she'd likely do it just to make him happy.

Gabe's smile widened. "You did? That's great. When are you going out on your first date?"

"Tomorrow night."

His smile, suddenly, took a downturn. He lifted her off his lap and placed her next to him.

"What's wrong?"

"I was going to see if you wanted to go out tomorrow night. I guess you have plans, now."

"I'm sorry, Gabe. You never mentioned anything. Besides, you wanted me to date Dean, right?"

"Of course. He'll be good for you." Gabe lifted off the couch and headed to the kitchen. Pulling on the long, vertical handle, he opened the refrigerator door and stared into it. "You have anything to drink around here? Some lemonade or something?"

She snorted. "Are you in a citrusy kind of mood?"

He mumbled under his breath. "Just need a distraction."

She lifted off the couch and sauntered toward him. Gracing him with a flirty smile, she tugged on his arm and said, "Thought I was your distraction. Or is it Marnie?" She giggled and then reached around him to grab the large pitcher toward the back of the fridge, only stopping when she felt his long, strong arms circle her waist and then pull her up. Letting go of the pitcher, she made a slight gasping sound when her back cradled into something solid, firm, and comfortably warm. Gabe nuzzled her neck and whispered. The warmth of his breath, across her bare skin, sent all kinds of heady, swirling sensations through her.

"You are, Arabelle." He gave her right butt cheek a quick swat and then walked away, leaving her mouth agape and her stunned.

He made his way back to the couch and stretched over it once again. "Now. Where is my lemonade?" He left the word "woman" out, knowing the misogynistic use of the word would've sent her into a tirade of emotion and her mouth spewing forth a sea of expletives for hours.

Her mouth still flapping open, she quickly closed it. She knew he was teasing her, playing caveman to her, current, domestic goddess role. Still, she'd give him attitude any chance she got. After squinting at him, she gave him a long, snide smirk before she grabbed two glasses from an overhead cabinet and took out the pitcher containing his favorite beverage.

She elongated the s in her reply. "Coming, *sir...*"

Placing everything on a tray, she balanced it on her way to the couch, dropping the tray gently in front of him with an elaborate sneer followed by a curtsy. He smiled, first, and then he chuckled.

CHAPTER 2

GABRIEL

Gabe's eyes went straight down to Arabelle's plump, round bottom as she bent over to grab the pitcher of lemonade. His irises viewed every edge, every delightful curve, until she swiveled toward him. To avoid getting caught, he popped his eyes, quickly, back up to her lovely, kind face while she poured the lemonade into separate glasses. He held his hand out to receive one before she split, making her way to the recliner off to one side of him. Thanking her, he took a few sips of the beverage before setting it onto a coaster.

"So, what are you doing for Thanksgiving?"

The holidays were a special time of year for him. For as long as they'd known each other, he and Arabelle always spent the holidays together. Even when they were dating others, they found time to set aside for the two of them. He loved this about their relationship. They were best friends for life.

At some point, they fell into an unspoken agreement. No matter what, they would make their friendship outlast all outside possibilities. Even if they both got married one day, they'd still remain best friends. They'd find the time to hang out with each other and catch up on their separate lives. Still, the idea of Arabelle marrying anyone unsettled his stomach and urged him to run far into the woods beyond his cabin. He did this, often, when he was confused, stressed, or when his inner beast demanded he expends energy. He never ran to get away from Arabelle. Never.

Revealing his shadow side to anyone was also something he never did. Sadly, this included Arabelle- the one woman whose opinion he prized highly. He knew one day he'd have to tell her what he truly was. He worried for her reaction when that day finally came. He supposed that was the main reason why he never shared his secret.

Each time he considered letting her know, a plethora of images filled his brain, alerting him to the real possibility of losing her. He'd sigh, long and low with regret and then cast the thought aside in favor of concentrating on something else.

Whenever that fateful day came, she'd make one of two choices. She'd either run from him or learn to accept him. He feared the former.

Arabelle had the worst luck when it came to men. Every time a man broke her heart, Gabe was there for her. Every-single- time. It didn't matter what he was doing. If she needed him, he was there for her. It was a fact several of his girlfriends found themselves uncomfortable with. Still, Arabelle came into his life first, and she'd remain.

He was fortunate to have Arabelle as a best friend, and he knew it. Sweet, kind, caring, honest, and loyal, there weren't many women like her. She'd go out of her way to help a stranger, often times running into restaurants or supermarkets to help buy a meal for a homeless person when others looked away. Just picturing Arabelle warmed Gabe's insides through and curved up the corners of his mouth. He definitely, won the lotto when she walked into his life.

"What are you smiling about, silly?"

Only then did he realize the goofy grin he sported on his face, all because of her.

"Just thinking of how you help the homeless. Do you have a charity project in mind this year for Christmas? I'd love to help you. We could buy gifts for the little angels' charity like we did last year. That was fun."

"I don't know... I'm thinking about it. I know I'll be doing something, but I'm not sure what, yet."

"Well, count me in, whatever you do. So, what about Thanksgiving?"

Arabelle gave him a sweet smile. "I thought I was going to your place?"

He nodded. "Good. Bring your date."

"But- I don't know if we'll be together."

"Of course, you will. I'm cooking the turkey so bring a dish to share. Marnie's coming too. She's bringing the green bean casserole and her lovely self."

Arabelle rolled her eyes. "Whatever. I don't need to hear about your love life. Just make sure she doesn't have too much to drink, so she doesn't spoil your evening plans."

Gabe winked. "I'll hide the liquor."

***

The next evening, Gabe couldn't help himself. He had to find out how Arabelle's date was going. He knew Dean was a good match for her, but he worried Arabelle might find fault with some of his lesser-known qualities. She was searching for Mr. Perfect. No matter how many times Gabe explained to her Mr. Wonderful didn't exist, she wouldn't revise her search parameters. His fingers flew over the phone's keyboard as he composed his message.

Thinking of you. How's the date? Do you need rescuing yet?

He placed the phone down next to him when a customer walked in. After taking the man's order and ringing him up on the register, he sauntered back toward the kitchen, where he informed his chef of what to make. He then walked toward the front of the store, when his phone sounded a familiar tune. He nodded at the cashier coming off a break and then glanced at the screen. It was Arabelle. She already discovered one of Dean's faults.

He chews loudly.

He snickered at her comment. Arabelle didn't like anyone who ate food with their mouth open. It was a pet peeve of hers. He figured if he chewed his food like that, they never would've been friends.

Remember, he's a good guy. Give him a chance.

Her reply came back faster than Gabe anticipated. Apparently, Arabelle excused herself from their table, or Dean did. She never would've texted Gabe while seated at the table.

I'm trying. Are you at the restaurant?

He answered with a smiley emoji. *When am I not?*

I'll pass by afterward.

He ended their chatter with an "okay," deciding, at the same time, to make something special for her since she was coming over. His pizza shop, which she gave the fancy title *restaurant,* served a limited menu. Yet, the food he served turned a decent profit.

Just then, a familiar face walked through the front door.

Marnie quickly strolled past the cashier and rounded the counter to where he stood. "Hey, babe."

"Hey yourself. What are you doing here?"

"I thought I'd grab you for a night out. So, what do you say? Come out with me. Let the staff do their job for once, instead of you."

He shook his head. "Can't. Arabelle's on her first date tonight with Dean. She's passing by here, afterward. Why don't you stay, and we can all enjoy a pizza or something?"

His eyebrows shot up with the snorting sound she made. "You spend way too much time with that woman."

He stared at her during the short, awkward silence, trying to figure out if she was sincere or trying to pass a joke made in poor taste. The staunch look on

Marnie's face led him to believe her comment wasn't comical. "That woman you're referring to is my best friend."

Marnie ran her hands down Gabe's chest and pouted. "So, you mean you can't go out with me tonight because of her?"

"She needs me."

"But I need you too! It's not fair. You spend all of your time with her."

"That's not true."

"I don't know what's so great about her anyway. She's just a friend."

"Best friend." He stared at her in disbelief. Why was she insulting Arabelle? Was she drunk, again? "I told you from the beginning how important Arabelle is to me. You said you understood."

"Well, I don't!"

"Marnie." He grabbed ahold of her arm and led her through the front door and out to one side of the shop for a bit of privacy. She shook out of his grip and squealed at him, in protest, when he didn't let her go.

"Listen. If you don't go out with me tonight, then we are over."

Gabe scrubbed a hand down the center of his face and, deeply, sighed. "Why are you doing this?"

"I don't want you around Arabelle anymore. I see how you look at her, how you regard her. You like her. You prefer her company over anyone else's. Just admit it."

He shook his head. "No, it's not true. I like you, Marnie."

"Then go out with me tonight."

He pointed back at the pizza shop. "I told you, I can't. She's meeting me here. Besides, you know how important my shop is. Why can't you just stay here and be with me?"

"But I won't be with you. I'll be with you, both."

"But Marnie, I'm going home with you. Why are you getting so upset about this?"

Marnie took a step back and pointed at him. "Because you like her. Admit it!"

He threw his hands up in the air and shouted. "Of course, I like her. I've known her for a very long time. She's my best friend, for crying out loud. Stop this, Marnie. This is ludicrous."

"I'll say it again. Tell her that you have other plans and then come out with me."

"No. I can't."

"Then we're over."

He combed his fingers through the thick hair atop his head. "Damn it, Marnie, if that's the way you want it, then fine. We're over. I won't have you giving me impossible ultimatums, and I won't have you disrespecting my best friend, ever."

Marnie swiveled on her heel and walked away. "Goodbye, Gabe."

He lowered his shoulders and sighed. What in the hell did he just do? He really liked Marnie, but she was being...*being*.... He didn't have the words. She'd never acted this way before. What got into her? Maybe she'd think about what she did and what she said. Maybe she'd change her mind. Would he take her back? After her display, he didn't know.

Right now, he had a shop to run and customers to take care of. He also had a few snacks to create for Arabelle- that's if she was still hungry by the time she arrived. Regardless, she could take them home with her. She always liked the food his establishment made.

Arabelle. Images of her beautiful brown eyes and her kind smile flickered in his mind. To think, Marnie implied he had a thing for Arabelle. How crazy. Arabelle was cute, funny, and sexy as hell too. Any man would be lucky to have her by his side. Yet, she'd never settle for Gabe. With a kind soul and a good heart, she deserved a man who'd treat her like a queen. Gabe could give her that, yet they were just friends. Best friends. Still, Gabe never considered anything beyond friendship with Arabelle. She was too good for him.

Okay... Maybe he wasn't being quite honest with himself. The fact was Gabe pictured Arabelle, on several occasions, in ways no friend ever should. He said she was sexy as hell, and he meant it. She had curves on her that had him pining at night for her body. The way she looked and carried herself, coupled with her remarkable beauty inside, had his dominant self, panting and drooling like a kid with a load of cash in a candy store. Yes. He wanted her. Yet, he worried for how long. She was a true gem. She deserved someone who'd treat her with the utmost care. A man who'd take her out to all the fancy restaurants, fly her anywhere in the world she wanted to go, and bring her every delicacy she desired. She didn't need a man with a pizza shop, a roving eye, and a secret only his parents knew.

During those special moments, she caught his fancy with a sexy wink, a slip of her pink tongue across her saucy lips, or a spontaneous snort of cute, girly laughter, Gabe would contemplate what it'd be like to be in bed with her, naked and vulnerable. If they ever found themselves in that situation- He closed his eyes as his heartbeat raced with the wild images.

Arabelle was special. She deserved more.

He wouldn't ruin her with him.

CHAPTER 3

ARABELLE

Hey," Arabelle greeted Gabe as soon as she stepped through the pizza shop's front door.

Gabe winked and took her coat, placing it behind the counter on a coat rack specifically set aside for employees. "Hey, belly."

"Oh god, I hate that nickname. Can't you call me something else?"

"What would you like, instead?"

She wrinkled her nose and pretended to go through words in her head. "I don't know. Guess I'll have to think of something. Where's Marnie? I thought she'd be with you."

"Marnie and I broke up."

Arabelle's jaw dropped. She stared at him. "What? When?"

He glanced back at his employees before he shuffled them off to one side of the counter, taking several steps toward the dining area. "About an hour and twenty, or so, minutes ago."

Arabelle followed him. "Oh no. I'm so sorry, Gabe. But why? I thought you were into her."

He grabbed ahold of her hand and led her toward a corner booth. "Difference of opinion."

"I'm so sorry," she said, sliding into one side of the booth while Gabe sat opposite of her. "Do you want me to go? What happened? If it's okay for me to ask."

He shook his head. "I want you to stay right there, and no, I don't want to talk about it."

She reached over the table and grabbed his hand. "You know, if you ever want to, talk that is, I'm here for you. I mean, you've always been there for me with my ex-boyfriends."

He gave her a quick smile. "Yeah, I know. Thanks. Sooo... how did the date turn out? Did you give Dean a chance?"

She wrinkled her nose and pouted. "I tried. I don't know. He seems like a nice guy, but most of the time, he was on his phone."

"On his phone? Doing what? Making phone calls?"

"Just texting someone. Then he took two calls. He left the table each time. I don't know who it was that called him."

"Maybe it was urgent. Did he say?"

"No. I didn't ask. I just thought it was rude. I mean, while I was talking to him, he was texting whoever it was. Don't you think that's kind of strange? I mean, it felt like he didn't care about me."

"But he likes you."

"He sure didn't show it tonight."

"Did he, at least, pay for dinner?"

"Nuh-uh. We paid our own separate checks."

Gabe half-lifted out of his seat. "What! I can't believe it. He said he liked you. I'm going to have to have a long talk with him when he gets back."

"No. Please. Don't worry about it. It's okay. Well, actually, it's not okay, but I don't want you making a big fuss. He wants to see me again, but I don't know...."

Gabe scratched his chin. "No. Not after he treated my girl like that."

She tilted her head to one side and snorted. "Um, I think that's my decision to make, ol' protective best friend of mine."

He chuckled. "I can't help it. I want the best for you."

"And the best I will have, on my own terms, if that's okay with you," she teased.

He raised his hands in the air in mock surrender. "Okay, okay. I know when I'm defeated. Hey... I have a good idea. Why don't you invite him over for Thanksgiving dinner at my place?"

She leaned forward. "Are you sure?"

Gabe gave her a single, slow nod. "Yeah, that way, I can keep an eye on him."

Arabelle leaned back into the padded bench when their server came over with the pitcher of water. After taking their drink orders, he returned shortly afterward with the garlic knots and garden salads Gabe, specifically, ordered for them. Arabelle extended her appreciation to the server and then to Gabe.

"This is so nice of you. Thanks."

"I hope you're still hungry."

She shoved a garlic knot into her mouth, bit down, and sighed. Her eyelashes fluttered dramatically. "Mmmm, I'm always hungry for your knots."

Gabe shifted in his seat. She could've sworn she heard a slight groan. She glanced at him curiously as he cleared his throat. "I should've had the cook make more."

"No, eight is quite enough. I'm glad you're sharing them with me."

"Well, don't get too full. I had the chef make your favorite Margherita pizza."

"Oh, Gabe... this is too much. Really."

He winked. "Nothing's too much for my girl."

She smiled. "You really are sweet. Thanks, bestie." She took another bite of her garlic knot while Gabe concentrated on his salad.

"So, since Marnie's not coming, do you want me to make the green bean casserole instead?"

He looked up from his salad. His eyebrows furrowed together. "And not bring your mashed potatoes? Hell no."

She laughed. "It's just from a box. I don't know why you like them so much."

"It's the way you make them. You always add some type of sparkle to it. It's like magic. When I make it, it's not the same."

She quipped. "I think you just like me, and that's why you like my mashed potatoes."

"Yeah, that too."

She grinned as she brought a forkful of salad to her lips and then pushed back from the table as the server dropped their drinks off. Shortly afterward, he returned with the pizza, placing the pedestal stand directly between them. She whipped around it to smile at Gabe.

"This looks so freakin' delicious. You really are spoiling me tonight. I'm not sure I can eat much else, though." Her gaze dropped down to her leafy plate. "I think once I get through the salad, I'm not going to have much of an appetite afterward."

Gabe lifted his hand in the air and waved the server forward. "You want him to wrap it up for you?"

Arabelle reached for Gabe's arm and lowered it. "Wait. I want to stare at it for a while and sniff the aroma."

Gabe laughed. "You go ahead and sniff away. Then we'll have it wrapped up with the zeppoles I had the chef make for you."

"Oh no! Oh my god, you didn't. I love those. I think I can wolf those down after the salad. But let me have something healthy, first, to combat the fat and calories." She giggled.

Gabe's tone of voice took a serious turn. He eyed her. "You don't have to worry about your weight."

"Only you would say that. You don't have to worry if you ever get a beer gut. Girls will still love you."

He spun the empty fork in his hand, first left then right, gazing at it as he spoke. "The only girl I care about loving me is you."

She gave him a cheesy grin. "I will always love you, Gabe. No matter what."

She swallowed down the rest of her lettuce as he locked his gaze with hers. "And I will always love you. I will always defend you. I will always protect you. I will always be your confidant."

"I know. I love that about you. And you know I'm here for you, always, Gabe. I love you so much."

He slowly ran his fingers across his chin as he regarded her.

"I'm glad you're my best friend."

Gabe broke eye contact and then changed the subject. They chatted for the next two hours before he closed the restaurant and sent his workers home. Gabe gave Arabelle a long, crushing hug standing outside the pizza shop. He released her minutes later. It was strange, but she sensed an immediate loss when they parted. It was as if her body was, somehow, only made for his. Molding perfectly into him, the idea of separating the two was wrong. She hadn't, seriously, considered anything beyond friendship with Gabe in a very long time, and the memory of that day at the football game threatened fresh tears in the corners of her eyes. She blinked them back before they had a chance to surface.

She changed the subject and kidded him about silly things, chatting about subjects that interested them both. All the while, he listened and gazed upon her intently, as if her words mattered and were the very thread his life relied upon.

She loved these moments. They were simple and pure, but they were also fun and exciting. The small chats, banter, and meaningful, deep conversations they shared made all the difference in her life. Gabe was a good friend. It's all he'd ever be.

After making a quip about all the food she was taking home and comparing the boxes to a mini buffet, she lifted up onto her tiptoes to give Gabe a peck on the cheek. He straightened back, and she hesitated, her eyes widening a bit, wondering what she should do next. Then he relaxed and allowed the chaste, friendly kiss, taking a bit too long to return the gesture on her left cheek before letting her go.

He called out to her seconds after she left his side. When she turned to him, she caught him shaking his head, his right hand doing the same in the air in front of him.

He dropped his head. "Never mind. Have a good night, Belly."

She smiled. She still hated that name.

CHAPTER 4

GABRIEL

Hours later, Gabe strode through the front door of his cabin. Deciding on a home in Tennessee wasn't an easy decision. His kind, normally, chose either a log cabin or a house in the remote woods. Yet, Gabe was different. He didn't jump to conclusions, and he didn't like fitting into the norm. He wanted something that matched his personality. Although he chose the traditional choice of log cabin his kind gravitated to, he added his own design to the inside, picking modern yet comfortable furniture over flannel and rugged, wooden discomfort. He strove for independence, simple luxury, and practicality. He also decorated his home with Arabelle in mind, allowing her to choose some of the statues and artwork displayed. He liked that her fashionable choices and impressions were noticeable within his domicile. It offered him a sense of comfort during those few, long nights without her. The cabin also offered him a safe space to observe the majestic mountains and the forest beyond. It gave him quick access to the means for his serenity and his need to escape when life became too stressful.

Gabe quickly changed out of his work clothes, tossing them aside for shorts, a muscle t-shirt, and running shoes. Grabbing his sports bottle and keys, he whipped out the door for his hiding spot -a medium-sized rock, ten miles past his cabin, where he hid his basic necessities when he was enjoying the simple pleasures of Mother Nature.

As soon as he reached his destination, he searched his immediate area for nosy passersby. He found glorious, peaceful stillness, instead. People didn't come here. It was too far up in the mountains, away from noisy civilization and retail stores. Gabe drew a long whiff of the place and smiled. Taking in his surroundings, he glanced at the tall, almost leafless trees, the rocky, sometimes treacherous terrain, and the crisp, mottled brown grass and sighed. He loved it here. Lifting his arms overhead, he pulled his shirt off, then his trunks, and kicked off his sneakers. He pushed the rock mere inches forward and noted a few ants crawling underneath it. Swishing them aside with his hand, he dug his fingernails into the Earth. He hollowed out a shallow grave, pulling from beneath the soil a large plastic bag containing his personal items. Brushing off the caked in dirt- likely muddied from random snow flurries during this time of year-he pulled apart the enclosure and stashed his clothes, sneakers, and keys into the bag, storing within it the sports bottle in an additional empty, waterproof container tucked inside. Zipping it closed for good measure, he placed it back into the ground, shifting the boulder over it to hide the contents while he played.

Next, he lifted his arms in the air, drew in a deep, satisfying breath, and shifted. Black fur dotted across his arms and back, replacing human hair. His nails grew longer, thicker, and curved at each end. His nose flattened into a snout, and his face stretched and elongated till his eyes almost disappeared. His small, sensitive ears curved up high on each side of his head. He fell to all fours. His beast grunted and stretched out his legs, more comfortable in this position versus standing. If Arabelle saw him now. What would she think?

He shook his large, rounded body to acclimate it to the sudden drop in temperature. The higher the elevation, the colder it was. It was easiest to tolerate when in motion or when properly clothed. Throwing his head back, he roared long, blissful seconds before he took off into the dense, thick, lush forest. At first, he lumbered, enjoying the crunching of the brown to black colored leaves underneath his paws. Yet, after some time, he grew bored with the repetition of step-crunch-step-crunch. He broke into a run, moving as fast as he could to expel all the frustrated energy trapped inside of him. Would Arabelle accept him? Would she love his furry form?

He staggered to a halt, pawed at the ground, snorted, and then snarled as he pictured her. His Arabelle. The one woman whose opinion would easily shatter him into a billion, tiny, microscopic pieces. It was likely the reason he never told her. Not because he didn't have the chance to. But because one critical look from her would devastate him. Completely destroy him.

He dropped onto the ground, emitting satisfied grunts as he rolled over patches of dirty grass and dead leaves, embedding into his skin all the wonderful smells surrounding him. He only stopped when all four paws were up in the air. Then he lowered onto his right side and lay there, happily, for several minutes as he pondered his sweet Arabelle. What was he going to do with her?

His head jerked up when he caught an unusual sound several miles away. His nose wrinkled with the raw musky scent he was all too familiar with. He scrambled to a stand, bounding his heavy weight up as fast as gravity allowed. Then he booked it, knowing if he didn't leave now, he'd either end up the subject of several photographs and social media posts or strung across a pit roasting over coals, the main course of a tasty dinner. Neither option appealed to him. He sprang through sporadic bushes and pounced between trees to safety.

CHAPTER 5

ARABELLE

Navigating the few stairs leading up to the front door of the log cabin while balancing the bottle of champagne in one hand and the warm bowl of mashed potatoes in the other was a challenge, she didn't plan for. Thank goodness Gabe lived in a single-story home. There'd be no more climbing stairs after her stellar, balancing performing act was done. As soon as she approached the door, she heard a whooshing sound. Two hands reached out and grabbed at the bowl of mashed potatoes.

She gave the familiar face, greeting her, a surprised look. "Oh! How did you know I was here? Were you waiting for me?"

"I was alerted by the sound from my video doorbell."

She rolled her eyes and then gave him

a playful smile. "Oh, I forgot you had one of those fancy things. We poor people don't have such luxuries."

He tweaked her nose with a low chuckle and grabbed the champagne bottle out of her hand, too. "Thank you for bringing this, though you didn't have to."

"It's okay. It's a celebration."

"So, is Dean coming? I thought he'd be with you?"

"He's coming separately. I wasn't sure how this get-together would go with him, so I wanted to make sure I could escape, just in case."

Gabe snorted as he pulled open the oven door to check on the turkey cooking inside. "Escape? You have me. There's no reason to escape. You can stay here, anytime you need to."

She nodded. "Thanks, Gabe." She ran to the door as the doorbell sounded. "That has to be Dean."

He stirred the corn on the stovetop. "Check, first. I don't want any strangers in my home."

She pulled the door open, greeting Dean with a swooshing sound. "Hey. These are for you." He shoved a bouquet of flowers at her, dumping them into her arms seconds before he shot past her into the kitchen. She gaped at the lovely arrangement of chrysanthemums, marveling at the array of colors, and then closed the door behind her.

Gabe eyed her as she walked into the kitchen to find a vase. He motioned toward the living room. "There's one in the China cabinet. That should fit. Dean, you can place that in the refrigerator. Thanks for bringing it."

"Sure, no problem." Opening the refrigerator door, Dean slipped the apple pie onto one of the shelves and then closed the door. He then hovered over Arabelle as she worked with the arrangement, placing the long stems, one by one, into the tall, crystal vase.

Dean whispered by her left cheek. "How've you been?"

"I've been good," she said, not taking her eyes off the flowers. The way his warm breath caressed the side of her neck sent shivers up her spine that stopped when she drew in a whiff of a strange odor.

The odor returned when Dean spoke again. "I've missed you." She stepped away from him, slowly and gradually so as not to alarm him. Dropping the flowers onto the counter, she grabbed a glass from the cabinet and offered to get Dean a beverage. He thanked her as he made his way to the sofa in front of the T.V. She brought him a glass of iced tea and breathed out a small sigh of relief when she returned to the kitchen. The guy was certainly handsome, but he must've not been aware of the state of his breath.

While she finished the flower arrangement, she split her time between entertaining Dean and hanging around Gabe. As a guest, she knew it was proper manners to try to assist the cook in any way, but she also hung around him so that she could swipe bits of gravy and "taste test" the corn and stuffing, too. She kidded with Gabe that her duty was to make sure the meal came out right. He only snickered at her efforts between long looks at her across the kitchen when she wasn't paying attention. The few times she caught him, he corrected himself and returned his focus to the stove or the oven, whichever one he should've been concentrating on at the moment.

As usual, Gabe already had the place settings on the dining room table. All that was left was the food. The grand finale happened shortly afterward. Dean and Arabelle took turns delivering food items in abundance from the kitchen to the dining room.

With Gabe sitting at the head of the table, Arabelle took the chair across from Dean. She sighed as she sunk into the seat, taking a few blissful seconds to marvel over the sumptuous meal Gabe had, mostly, prepared. Grabbing a knife and fork, she dug into her first taste of the juicy turkey, laughing when Gabe pointed out the dribble escaping her mouth and running down her chin. She swiped it with a napkin before complimenting the chef on the tenderness of the meat. For as long as she'd known Gabe, he'd always done a great job in preparing the holiday meals. Plus, he enjoyed cooking them- a bonus in her book as creating multiple delicacies over a hot stove wasn't exactly her idea of fun.

Gabe and Arabelle regaled jovial tales from their past while Dean and Gabe shared their own comical customer moments from the pizza shop. When all the dishes were cleared from the table, they settled around the fireplace and chatted some more, playing a few card games to while away the time. After losing for the fifth time, Arabelle begged off any more games to Gabe's deliberate wink.

"Sore loser?"

"Just because you're winning...." She left her sentence hanging. Crossing her arms in front of her, she gave Gabe a playful pout. He chuckled and shuffled the cards once more.

Dean won the next round, and Arabelle cheered. In the middle of their celebratory hug, Gabe suggested a game he purchased recently for them to try.

The sudden awareness that Gabe bought a board game without her knowledge punched her low in the gut. It was silly of her to worry. She knew it. Yet the fact was they shared everything. When did Gabe buy the game? Why didn't he tell her? Why didn't he bring her with him to purchase whatever it was he bought? She silently chastised herself. Stop. Gabe didn't do it on purpose. Just stop. What in the hell was wrong with her? She looked at Gabe as he awaited her answer.

Lowering his voice, he took a step toward her. Somehow, sensing her concern, he murmured a response. "I just purchased it this morning from a retail store along the way. I didn't want to bother you to come out with me. I knew you were busy preparing the mashed potatoes. And you *know* how important those mashed potatoes are to me."

She snorted. "I'm sorry, Gabe."

"It's okay. I saw the look." He smiled. "Come play the game with us. It'll be fun."

The colored dots spread out across the white background seemed confusing at first. For a brief second, Arabelle wondered if Gabe ever played the game with Marnie.

During their first attempt, Gabe let Arabelle and Dean tackle the mat while standing off to one side and playing referee. The scene was hilarious until she toppled over Dean, who, suddenly, became very handsy. She squirmed her way off him and rocketed off the flimsy mat, attempting to stand when her traitorous right foot slipped, and she collapsed back onto it. Her hands flung wildly in the air to keep her footing. She grimaced and then yelped out loud when she landed hard on her back.

Gabe immediately tossed the spinner board to the side. He rushed to her aide while Dean called out to her.

Gabe grabbed her upper arm. "Are you okay?" He slipped his hand into hers as he attempted to lift her. He stopped when she sucked in air through her front teeth.

His eyebrows furrowed. "You're hurt."

"I'll be okay. Just give me a minute."

Gabe shook his head. "I should never have bought this game. I just thought it would be fun for us to play."

"It's okay, Gabe. Really." Dean grabbed her other side, and together they lifted her to a seating position.

After receiving aspirin and a glass of water, Arabelle took them readily from Gabe and thanked him for the kind offer.

Gabe retrieved the glass from her hand. "You want to sit on the couch?"

"No, I'm good. Let's play one more game. It's kind of fun, actually. I've never played Twister before."

"Neither have I," Gabe confessed.

"I'll be the referee this time," Dean offered.

Gabe smiled wide. "Great. I get to play against my best friend."

Arabelle teased, "Get ready to lose."

Gabe snickered. "Not if you fall, first. Just kidding." He held his hands out by his sides in a gesture of surrender.

Her second attempt at the game proved adventurous. Gabe and Arabelle shared bursts of laughter, watching as the other twisted their bodies into impossible pretzel-like shapes all to cover a color. Dean shouted from a safe distance at the edge of the mat. Arabelle went in one direction while Gabe went in another. It was all pretty manageable and organized until Dean shouted out the color green.

Gabe placed his right hand on the spot next to Arabelle. Impossibly leaning his broad upper chest closer to her smaller frame, he, somehow, steadily, kept his left hand on the blue circle behind her. The strong contours of his statuesque facial features hovered mere inches above her, and his warm breath ushered from his soft, kissable lips teased and mingled with hers. Arabelle found it hard to concentrate. If she wanted Gabe, all she had to do was pounce- literally- and she'd have him.

She rolled her eyes and closed her eyelids with a silent sigh as his earthy scent tantalized her nostrils. The familiar, comfortable mix of sandalwood and evergreen threatened to weaken her knees. She was ready and more than willing to admit defeat if only Gabe was the prize awaiting her...

Her body yearned for him. Her nipples tightened. Her even-keeled breaths struggled in keeping their easy tempo as she realized his face was mere split seconds away from hers. She found herself staring into gentle, brown eyes that, suddenly, blinked. His long, lush eyelashes swept upwards, and then a toothy grin appeared. She knew she should look away but, somehow, she couldn't. All she could do was gape, longingly, at the one man she wanted for her own.

Dean said something, reminding her that he, too, was present in the room. Why in the hell was she pining over Gabe, again, when Dean was a great contender? Yet, she had always loved Gabe, and Gabe had rebuffed her a long time ago. She'd never gotten over it. Dean repeated whatever he said before. Yet, Arabelle didn't hear the next color, nor did she seem to care.

"Arabelle? Are you okay?"

Gabe asked her the question. Was

she truly alright? Fixated on Gabe's beautiful eyes, she wasn't aware of much else. She didn't want anything else. The moment was absolutely perfect. Yet, she wasn't prepared for what happened next.

Gabe leaned toward her. Instinctively, she closed her eyes, though, in hindsight, she wondered what possessed her to think that was okay. This was Gabe- her best friend- not her lover. Still, Gabe had every opportunity to back away. He had the chance to watch her open her eyes, pop out a quick joke, and question why her eyelids were closed and what she expected from him. Then everything would return to normal. Instead, he placed his soft lips on her, and he kissed her.

Giddy pleasure sprayed over her like a pleasant, perfect perfume, blanketing her brain with swirling sensations she had never felt before. Somewhere in the background, she overheard Dean shouting, demanding answers to what was happening. Yet Arabelle didn't have any. She opened her eyes to find Gabe's mouth still on hers. At some point, in the middle of their kiss, he abandoned the small circles on the mat. He was now kneeling on the floor, cupping the back of her head with his hands and seeking entrance into the sweet cavern of her mouth. She closed her eyes again and succumbed, willingly, to his demands. Opening her mouth to his eager exploration, she allowed him to tease and taunt her into submission. Their hands intertwined and then wrapped around each other quickly. She sighed into his mouth when he, eventually, ended their kiss. Then he stared at her wide-eyed as she struggled to breathe. Everything she wanted happened. Yet the shocked look across Gabe's face told her he regretted what they did.

Dean yelled. "What in the hell is this?"

Gabe lifted from the floor and placed his hands out in front of him. "I don't know."

Arabelle shied away from the two males and rose to a stand. There was no valid or sound explanation for what occurred. She only wanted to disappear.

Dean shook his head. "I can't believe what I just saw. I think we're done. With Thanksgiving and everything. I'm outta here." Dean grabbed his coat.

"I'm sorry." Her apology was drowned out by the slam of the door. Her shoulders slumped forward. She regretted hurting Dean. Yet her attraction to Gabe had always been there. She figured what they did was bound to happen sooner or later. It was only now she realized that it wasn't what Gabe wanted.

Arabelle snuck a peek at Gabe and found him in the kitchen. Instead of talking to her or processing with her what occurred, he picked up a dish in the sink and acted as if nothing had happened.

"Do you need help?" She called to him from the doorway. Gabe shook his head. Pouring soap onto a sponge, he let the water run over the dish in his hand before he scrubbed it.

She sauntered closer, looking at him over the edge of the counter. "Well, do you want to talk about the kiss?"

He snorted as he shoved the plate into the dish rack. Then he grabbed another from the sink. "No. It was a mistake. I'm sorry."

He jerked his head up with her short laugh. "Well, I guess Dean was right. Thanksgiving is over. I'll see you later, Gabe."

Anger rose within Arabelle's gut as she grabbed at her purse. She'd known Gabe all her life. She should've expected his behavior. Yet, she thought, this once, the outcome might be different. It was typical Gabriel. It was just like him to ignore the elephant in the room instead of addressing it. She stomped toward the exit taking brief seconds to glance over her shoulder at him, disappointment setting within her eyes before she opened his front door. "Thank you for dinner. It was really nice. Take care of yourself."

She spotted his eyebrows furrowing together and caught a look in his eyes she'd never seen before. Was it want or desire? Whatever it was, he didn't act on it. Instead, he watched her close the door behind her and walk away.

CHAPTER 6

GABRIEL

What in the hell possessed him to kiss her? Arabelle must've worked some strange magic on him or something. That was the only explanation. She looked cute, all flushed, and bent over the mat next to him, her arms struggling to keep her body parts from making contact with his. He loved the thrill, enjoyed the rush. He remained amused at her staunch effort to remain upright and as separate, from him, as possible. Still, that was no excuse to take advantage of the one woman who meant so much to him.

After the kiss that changed his entire world, he didn't know how to face her now. What could he say to her to explain his impulsiveness? That he always wondered what it was like to kiss her. That he was sating a mere curiosity. That it was the most amazing, perfect kiss he'd ever received? He'd never admit it.

Now that he knew what her lips tasted like, he wanted more. Kissing her was unparalleled to anything he had ever experienced. Her lips were incredibly soft, sweet, and a perfect match for his. He yearned for another taste, this time in a more intimate setting of their choosing. When he felt Arabelle's shoulders and body un-tense in his arms- He wanted to shout in celebration. Her submission to his beast's darker needs was the most incredible sensation. Re-living the glorious seconds had the front of his pants tenting and yearning for more.

His hidden beast- a secret he held from her- knew the truth as soon as his lips touched hers. She was his fated mate. Yet, he didn't want to believe it. He didn't want to acknowledge it, for it couldn't be true. She was meant for another, not him.

Who Arabelle was destined to be with, he didn't know. What he did know was that she wasn't meant for Dean. That was all too clear tonight when she jerked away from him and almost hurt herself in her effort to escape his close proximity in the first game she played. She didn't do that with Gabe. She didn't even flinch when he caressed her beautiful bare shoulder with his warm breath. He teased her, on purpose, awaiting a reaction. What came next felt natural, comfortable, and, damn it, if he didn't enjoy himself!

Yet, Arabelle accomplished her goal in the end. She fled. Only, she left *Gabe*, not Dean. Scampering out of his log cabin, she departed Gabe's company. He growled low, uncaring if his neighbors heard his animal side or not. He gripped the bowl in his hand. The intense desire to fling the ceramic object across the room and watch it smash into a gazillion tiny little pieces urged him to sate his desire for destruction. Drawing in several deep breaths, he tamped down the dark urges swirling about in his brain. Suppose he didn't demolish everything in his home. In that case, he'd run out, find Arabelle and drag her back to his cave, albeit his cabin, for some desirable, one on one time. He slowly enunciated her name. Each syllable slipping over his tongue invited salacious ideas into his head. He wanted her, but he couldn't have her. She wasn't his mate. He couldn't believe sweet, kind, beautiful, one-of-a-kind Arabelle was meant for him. She was too good for him. He'd never be enough for her.

Gabe swiveled to his right, growled aloud, and then swung his right fist straight through the wall.

***

After what happened back at his cabin, Gabe assumed Dean would take a day or two off from work. Yet, leaving him in the lurch on the busiest day of the year? He held back the urge to pick up the phone and fire him on the spot. His little pizza shop almost couldn't keep up with the hustle of November twenty-sixth. It seemed between black Friday shopping spots, patrons slipped in for a snack or an entire meal, filling up their bellies before hitting the road again in search of more bargains.

Gabe was more than certain Dean remained upset at the crazy incident that occurred on Gabe's living room floor with Arabelle. Still, he didn't give Gabe a chance to explain himself. After last night's fiasco, he rehearsed what he'd say to Dean today. Yet, he didn't show up. Gabe was about to tell him that what happened last night was unplanned, unexpected, and never to be repeated, again. He'd vouch for Arabelle feeling the same way and beg Dean to give her another chance. There was no way Dean was giving up on Arabelle because of Gabe's loose lips that happened to find themselves on Arabelle's sweet, delectable, and delightful mouth.

Recollections of their kiss intruded, sending pleasure signals straight to his groin. Gabe grumbled as he hid his lower half behind a counter from a customer's view. He cashed out the patron and then exchanged roles with a nearby staff member, taking advantage of the opportunity to slip out of sight. Back in his office, he chastised himself for the images he projected in his head that would never come to fruition. They had one kiss. That was it. Nothing would ever come of it.

Last night was the worst night of his life. His brain wouldn't stop replaying every second of their joyful kiss. At several points, he leapt up from the bed to either splash water on his face, step into the tub to take a cold shower with and without his pajama pants, or rub one-off and then go back to bed. It was the latter he enjoyed, having indulged in self-pleasure about eight times last night, shouting her name with each blissful ending. He had to stop envisioning Arabelle naked. In the last six hours, he had imagined Arabelle in every position he'd taken former girlfriends in. Yet, there was only one particular position he reserved for his mate.

He branded that image into his memory six out of the eight times he took himself in his hand. Arabelle was in a soapy, water-filled tub slipping down onto him. Facing him, at first, he then flipped her to ride him reverse cowgirl style. He watched her bounce up and down, issuing guttural groans to her moans of delight. Next, he slipped into her from behind while she hung over the edge of the tub, her fingers gripping the sides for support as he stroked harder. Reaching around her to tease her clit, he caressed her everywhere she liked, calling out her name to his completion. They languished in the tub afterward.

Hugging, kissing, caressing, and washing her naked body, in between their sexual encounters, had his groin aching, his cock lengthening, and his inner beast craving her once more. He'd never taken a shower, bath, or a bubble bath with any of his former dates. That was reserved for Arabelle, his mate- the one woman he'd never have. He growled, low. Then, he whipped his head toward the door, making sure no one heard him or approached his office.

Although Gabe wanted her, Arabelle was better suited to Dean. Gabe would let him know when he showed up. If he did.

The following scheduled workday, Dean left another voicemail, this time at five-thirty a.m. Gabe tried to hide the frustration whirling inside of him while a part of him demanded to know if Dean was looking for another job. He contemplated calling Dean. Instead, he picked up the phone, scrolled through his list of contacts, and pressed Arabelle's name. It had been four days since Thanksgiving, and she had not returned any of his calls. Where was she? What was she doing? She had never skipped out on returning his phone calls. After receiving her voicemail, he tossed his apron onto the counter in frustration and announced he was taking a long lunch break.

Stalking toward his car, he resolved to contact her again when he reached a stoplight. Gabe's hopeful attitude soured as soon as he heard her voicemail, once again. After driving more than ten minutes, he growled and then chuffed when his thoughts returned to Arabelle, his stubborn yet gorgeous best friend. Once he got his hands on her, he'd...he'd...take her down and make sweet love to her. No! Damn it, Gabe. Get it together. He silently chastised himself as randy thoughts filled his mind with tawdry images.

He mumbled under his breath as his grip tightened on the steering wheel. "Arabelle's your best friend. Not some cheap lay in the sack." He'd never treat her like some side piece. She was precious, genuine, and the real thing. Sex with Arabelle would be...indescribable. He rolled his eyes to the back of his head and uttered a sound much like intense pining or sad whimpering. Right now, he'd be happy with a warm hug or a friendly kiss on the cheek- neither which seemed options with her imposed silence. He grumbled under his breath while vivid images of Arabelle's sweet smile, her kind eyes, and her soft, curvy hips intruded. He'd do anything to hear her sultry lips, playfully, bantering with him, again. Instead of kidding or teasing him, as usual, she decided to remain mute. Once he reached her home, he'd have a long talk with her, possibly on the couch, in the kitchen, or on her bed, between her legs. No! Stop it. He wouldn't take her down like a piece of meat or devour her like delicious prey.

He shook his head, attempting to jolt out any lingering images regarding an intimate future with Arabelle. Then he smashed his foot down on the accelerator. No more messing around. It was time to face Arabelle.

When he reached her door, he knocked hard, ready to confront the one female who caused him unnecessary angst the last several days, not including several sleepless nights. He sniffed the door frame when she didn't answer. She was in there. He sensed her heartbeats hammering faster in her chest and heard her footsteps pacing across her laminate wood floor. She wasn't going to answer the door. Damn it! He knocked louder.

"Arabelle. I know you're in there. Answer the door." He growled low as he stared at the painted, wooden barrier separating them. Memorizing every detail, he found himself counting the individual panels and then re-counting them several times to make sure he had the total number correct as he waited for her next move. Yet, he knew how stubborn she was. He banged his fist against the door once more. "Arabelle. I want to talk to you. Open the door. I'm getting tired of looking at it." He closed his eyes and hung his head in resignation before he uttered the next few words. "I need you."

The door whooshed open. There stood Arabelle as radiant as ever. His eyes raked over her and widened as he took in her sad smile, her tear-filled eyes, and the clothing she wore that accentuated every curve. The graphic tee excited his brown irises and hugged her delectable breasts to perfection. Her whitewashed jean shorts came up mid-thigh high, giving Gabe ideas that tipped over the border to devilish.

She stood in the doorway and then nibbled on her lower lip. His gaze riveted to her mouth. "I'm sorry, Gabe."

He slowly sighed. "I missed you."

"I missed you, too. I just-didn't know

what to do."

"Talk to me. That's what you do." He pushed the door further in and stepped forward. His frame towered over her. At first, she didn't move. He breathed in her scent, delighting in the flowery musk-filled perfume that was unique to her. No other smelled like Arabelle. None ever would. Her natural perfume was her signature. A warm, cozy mix he'd welcome into his home every day. He only now realized how much he had missed it.

Instead of backing up or moving out of his way, she closed the gap between them. Falling softly against his chest, she murmured into it. "I'm sorry, again. I'm glad you're here. I really missed you. I'm sorry I didn't call you back." She folded her arms around him. He tilted her chin up as random tears fell from her eyes.

"Don't cry. And you don't need to apologize to me. Just be here for me. I'm here for you."

Lowering her head to rest on his chest, she squeezed her arms together, embracing him in a tight hug. "I know." He caught the start of a small smile and then groaned, in appreciation, as she rubbed her head, affectionately, across his shirt. Her delectable scent, her soft, curvy body, and her sweet lulling tone of voice were almost too much for him to bear. The effect of her was swift, sending satisfying jolts of pleasure straight to his groin. He shifted his hips at a safe, awkward angle before she detected his ardor for her.

Resting her head across his shoulder, tendrils of her straight hair fell randomly back as she looked up at him. Her eyes softened as she spoke the next few words. He caught the gentle, tender look within her irises. It stirred up something primitive within him.

"I love you."

Those three simple words shot straight through his heart. The impact jolted him out of her arms and knocked the wind out of him. He grabbed ahold of the door frame and leaned forward, trying to regulate his sudden, haphazard breathing.

"Gabe? Are you okay?" She clasped her hand around his upper arm. Pleasure zipped through him, causing goosebumps to skitter across his skin. He fought the urge to do more, a sense of urgency to claim and possess overtaking his muscles and nagging at him to slam the door behind them, locking it, permanently, closed.

"Gabe?"

He took one look at her. Catching the confused look in her eye and the concern pouring forth from her perfect, pink lips, his last chain of resistance broke. He lunged at her and pulled her fiercely into his arms. Crushing her lips to his, he growled out his need. Her eyes widened, and she placed her hands on his shoulders, pushing against him in an effort to free herself. Yet, she wasn't escaping. She had four days of solitary freedom, and that was enough. She was never leaving him again.

She sounded her protests and then silenced. Her shoulders softened, indicating to him her submission. His inner beast roared in victory, jubilation fueling his muscles with energy. His hands roamed over her body, caressing every inch of her curves to her moans of delight. He backed her through the doorway, flung his arm behind them, and slammed the door without letting her go.

"Gabe, Gabe, what are we doing?"

He twirled his fingers through her hair and smiled. "What I want to do. What we want to do."

She shook her head. "No."

"Why not?"

She shoved out of his arms. "You don't want this."

"Of course, I do."

A familiar sound interrupted them. Gabe slipped out his phone from his back pocket and glanced at the screen.

"Do you have to take that?"

He stared at it a few seconds longer

and contemplated. It was Marnie. What did she want? Whatever it was, she picked the wrong time to call him.

"You should take it. I'll be over here." She pointed to a leather love seat at the opposite side of the room with just enough room for them to finish what they started. He glanced back at the phone as the ringing started up again. For Marnie to call him a second time, it must be important. Still, he hesitated to take the call. Arabelle would use the interruption as a perfect excuse to change the subject. He'd never get the chance to re-visit the attraction they had for each other.

He grunted when Marnie sent him a text message.

Gabe. I need you. Please come by the house.

Damn. It was what he thought. What was he going to do?

He slipped the phone back into his pocket. "I'm sorry, I have to leave. But we're not done here."

"Oh? Is everything okay?"

"It's Marnie. An emergency."

Arabelle sauntered over to him. She slid the back of her hand, lovingly, down Gabe's left cheek. "Okay. I hope she's all right."

Grabbing ahold of her hand before it slipped off his chin, he growled. "I'm not done with you. Wait for me. We need to talk." He lifted her hand to his lips and planted a kiss onto it before he released it, grabbed the door handle, and walked away.

CHAPTER 7

ARABELLE

Arabelle watched as Gabe's firm butt and long legs left her home. What happened between them just now not only surprised her but confused her too. Gabe never held an interest in Arabelle- at least not in that way. Yet, here he was kissing her twice within days. It was strange, and she didn't know what to make of it. The only excuse she could fathom was the possibility of Gabe's break up with Marnie being too much for him to handle. Maybe he was lonely. Since she was his best friend, she was the easiest and most available means to ease his pain.

That was another thing. Marnie called him, and Gabe left. Yet, they weren't together anymore. However, Gabe was the type of man to come to someone's rescue. If anyone needed him, he always pulled through. Or at least he tried his very best to. Whatever happened to Marnie to warrant several phone calls to Gabe, she hoped, in the end, Marnie was okay. Gabe seemed a mess without Marnie. Maybe they'd get back together? The idea, though, didn't sit well with Arabelle, for some reason.

Above all else, she wanted Gabe's happiness. Yet, she had to protect herself, too. Gabe was often a flirt, a tease. One never knew what his agenda was. Even he confused her, sometimes. If the world remained perfect, Gabe would've ended up with her a long time ago. Yet things weren't perfect, and neither were they. The fact that Gabe wanted to start something with her, now... He'd, surely, break her heart in the end, for he'd find someone new. She wouldn't allow him to hurt her like that. She loved him too much to destroy what they had together.

Still, when Gabe called her the following day to inform her he was back with Marnie, her heart dropped into her stomach. She didn't expect the next words to come from his lips.

"I have to let you know we had sex."

Arabelle lost her grip on the phone. She watched as the phone slipped out of her fingers and headed to the floor. She attempted to grab it in mid-air but not having superpowers, she knew the attempt was futile. Instead, to her chagrin, she witnessed the phone spinning in the air and falling face down.

"Figures," she said, carefully scooping up the device and checking for cracks and chips in the screen protector. She gave a frustrated sigh when she heard Gabe call her name several times.

Locating the speakerphone icon, she pressed it. "Sorry, the phone slipped out of my hand. I'm okay."

"Are you sure?" Gabe remained silent for several long seconds. "Look, I wouldn't have said anything, but I feel bad after what happened last night at your place. I thought you deserved an explanation. Now that I'm with Marnie, again, I have to give us a try. Please understand."

"I do. I get it. It's okay. I just want you to be happy. Are you?"

"Of course."

"That's all I want, Gabe. Besides, you know you've been lost without her."

"Maybe. I'm sorry, Arabelle. "

"Why are you apologizing? We're friends, right?"

"Always but Marnie... You know how she feels about you. I'm going to try to put her first. That means you might not hear from me as often."

She swallowed down the dry lump forming in the back of her throat. The idea of not hearing from Gabe saddened her heart. He was always the one she went to when she wanted to share something funny, happy, or a good bit of gossip from her job. Now Gabe was telling her he wouldn't be around. Her breaths turned shallow, and something grabbed ahold of her heart and squeezed it. She had no idea what to say, what to think. Yet, whatever his decision, she'd support it. She had no other choice. He was her best friend.

"You know I'm here for you. No matter what."

"I know. Thank you, Arabelle. That means a lot to me. I gotta go now."

That was the last time she heard his charming, manly voice in a little over two weeks. Each time she considered reaching out to him, she reined back the desire, reminding herself that she had to give him his space. She'd let him contact her, instead. He knew if he needed her, she'd be there.

Yet, his text messages came in sporadically nowadays, and his phone calls were almost non-existent. Any messages he left were brief and to the point. He told her he missed her on countless occasions, but he said he was fine. He and Marnie were working things out. They were good. That brought a bitter-sweet smile to her face.

Instead of spending his extra time with her, he spent that time with Marnie. One weekend, he informed her they went off on a trip together. It was good. He was good. Arabelle heard the word *good,* so many times she wondered if it was true. Yet, she didn't ask him any questions. She didn't want to interfere. She only hoped he remained truly happy.

Still, the time he spent away from her proved painful. Arabelle got used to having him around. She supposed she took it for granted that he spent so much time with her. She wished she could go back in time and tell him how much it meant to her to have him sharing countless hours with her. She loved and enjoyed his company. Not having him in her life literally hurt. She spent too many nights crying into her pillow. Although he was still around, she lost her best friend. She knew it would happen, eventually, and she should've seen it coming. Still, she didn't expect or plan for the sudden change in their relationship and the painful intensity of her loss.

Living their new reality proved strange and increasingly uncomfortable. It was something she had to get used to. Still, when the third week of December crept up on her calendar, Arabelle knew she had to call him. Her heart stuttered when his gruff tone of voice caressed her eardrums.

She sighed into the phone. "Hey. It's so good to hear your voice. How have you been? How's Marnie?"

"Hi, Belly. We're good. How have you been?"

She snickered. "I'll let the nickname go just this once." She caught his roar of laughter. "I'm okay, but I'm wondering, can you still come with me to my office party on Friday? Did you want to? I know we made plans before, but now you have a girlfriend, so it's okay if you can't. I understand. I mean, we made plans way back when you were single, and you know you've come with me every year, but you don't need to this time. It's okay. Don't feel like you have to come."

She was rambling, and she knew it. Still, she didn't want him feeling obligated to attend. The idea of appearing, without him, at her annual holiday party seemed as unnatural as the current state of their relationship. However, a lot of things nowadays seemed upside down and different. Arabelle was a mere observer of Gabe's slow disappearing act. He didn't walk out of her life. He was, only, removing himself from the majority of it. Soon, one day, he'd completely disappear and leave Arabelle bereft and missing an essential part of her existence.

"I don't know. You know why Marnie and I didn't work out the first time. I'm trying to put her first, but I did make a promise to you, and I want to keep it. We always said we'd celebrate Christmas together. It's your favorite holiday, and I can't let you down. I'll talk to her. I'll let you know."

"I miss you, Gabe." The rest of the words she wanted to convey choked up in her throat. She bit her lip to keep her emotions from escalating and bubbling over. Instead, she remained silent and let the sudden tears fall. If only she could tell him the truth. Life wasn't the same without him. If he'd listen to her, she'd beg him to come back. She'd invite him over, if he wanted, and give him that kiss he sought and possibly more. Yet, he'd have to leave Marnie, and Arabelle couldn't ask him to do that. Not when he was trying so hard to make it work. Still, in a perfect world, Arabelle would be the only one for him. Gabe deserved so much. If she could, she'd give him the world.

"I miss you, too." She heard his sharp intake of air. "Quite a lot, actually. It's-it's really hard not being with you."

Her heartbeat kicked up several beats. "Gabe, please come with me to the office party."

"I'll try. I gotta go now. I'll get back with you. Hey, take care of yourself, okay."

"Yeah, you too. Please." A clicking sound indicated the end of the call. She closed her eyes, drew in several deep breaths, and then gave up. She blubbered into her hands and let the tears fall.

***

A few days later, while assisting a customer on the company's online communicator system, her cell phone vibrated. She flipped the device over to find Gabe's text message.

I'll see you Friday. Pick you up at seven?

Instant joy zapped through her heart. She, gleefully, grinned, excited at the prospect of seeing Gabe again. She made a small sound of happiness into the receiver of her headset and then apologized to the customer, letting them know her elation was a result of receiving good news. Now she had something to look forward to. She'd have to buy a perfect dress for the occasion.

After work, she scampered into one of her favorite retail stores, picked out a few outfits, and then tried them on. The worst part of being plus-sized was the limited selection of stunning designs. Granted, there were dresses on the rack. Yet, drop-dead gorgeous ones that complemented her generous figure? Nah. They were few and far between. If she found one, it was a heaven-sent miracle. Today must've been one of those rare occasions, for the last outfit she tried on was absolutely perfect.

She modeled the dress in front of the mirrors mounted on opposite walls of the small fitting room. Walking from one corner of the room to the other, she swished her shape right then left and checked each angle, pleased with what she found. The long slit on the left side of her dress started at the bottom and rode all the way up to her lower thigh, just above her knee. Her derriere, holding a bit more- what did they call it- junk in the trunk, jutted out nicely from the back of the dress. She had that and wide hips too. Yet, she was comfortable with her shape. She only wished the clothing companies were, too. Still, the black sequined dress with the low-cut cleavage was amazing. The sides of her waist sported black mesh cutouts- just enough to entice a viewer to want to know more. The garment was naughty, sexy, and really beautiful. Would Gabe take notice? Yet, he had Marnie. Just saying his girlfriend's name was like a wet towel slapping straight across her face. Maybe she shouldn't wear the dress after all and put it back on the rack where she found it.

She warred with herself whether to buy the dress or not. In the end, her scandalous, devilish side won out. She soon found herself at a cashier's station, tapping her card across the reader and then walking out of the store with her captivating purchase. Tempting Gabe wasn't her plan when she sought a suitable dress for the party. It was only an unexpected bonus. Witnessing Gabe's reaction would be priceless. Excited at her purchase and the prospect of seeing him again, she texted Gabe a quick message.

Just found a dress. Can't wait to see you again.

Her right index finger stayed in midair, hovering over the green arrow button, as she stared at her words. She couldn't send that. What if Marnie saw what she wrote? She deleted the second half of the text and added:

I'm ready for the party.

Satisfied, she pressed the arrow button and sent the message. If Marnie found her text message, he wouldn't get in trouble.

***

Her heartbeats thundered rapidly as

soon as she heard the knock on her door. She rushed to open it, banging the slab of wood hard against the inner wall, uncaring if it created any damage. Opening her arms wide, she shouted, "You're here!" She propelled herself into Gabe's arms to his boisterous laughter. He held her tight around the waist, twirling her in the air as they both heartily laughed. When he placed her feet back onto the floor, she had tears already rimming her eyes. She swiped at them when he reached out, grabbed her hand, and held it still.

"No, let me." His index finger gently wiped at several threatening to burst from the corners of her eyes. He stopped his attempt to clear her tears and, instead, raked his gaze, slowly, over her. "I forgot how beautiful you are."

She snorted. Grabbing onto his arm, she dragged him behind her through the open doorway. He shut the door behind them and then halted her attempts to move them forward. "No, I meant it. You are one gorgeous woman."

Arabelle playfully swatted at his upper arm. "Oh, stop. I don't think Marnie wants to hear that from you. Besides, you're the one that's beautiful. No wonder women can't stop falling in love with you."

He closed his mouth and regarded

her in the ensuing silence.

"Now, where is this dress you told me about? I thought you'd be wearing it."

"What? And spoil the surprise? I have my makeup and jewelry on, so all I have to do is slip on the dress, some shoes, and re-fix my hair, and I'm done. Wait right there for me." She pointed to the leather loveseat and scampered off into the bedroom before he had a chance to read the expression across her face. Glancing at the leather loveseat and then back at Gabe reminded her of the last time he visited her place, almost three weeks ago. It was an ugly memory, one she didn't care to remember. That night, after sharing a hot kiss with Gabe, he promptly left her and then had sex with Marnie. That was the night they got back together. If she had the ability to erase her memories, she'd wipe out that one in particular. It served her no purpose and only added to her grief.

After slipping on the dress, her heels, and fixing herself up, she poked her head out from the doorway and called out to Gabe. "Are you ready?"

He smirked. "I've been ready. At this point, you could go to the party in your birthday suit, and I'd be fine with that. Well...maybe not all that fine with it. I'd have to fend off all the men at the party." Arabelle could've sworn his nostrils flared.

"Well, here I come." She threw the bedroom door wide open and strode, confidently, through the living room. His eyes widened, and then his jaw dropped. She heard him inhale a sharp intake of air in the sudden silence. She smiled as she twirled in front of him, tightening her fingers around the glittery clutch in her hand as she attempted to maintain her poise in three-inch-high heels. As she closed the loop she formed on the floor in front of him, she couldn't help delighting in the fact that his gaze remained focused on her, his eyes hitting every area on her body a man's normally would.

She threw her arms out to her sides. "So, what do you think? You like it?"

He shifted his position on the couch and cleared his throat. "Damn, Arabelle. Wow."

"What? You don't like it?" she teased.

He gave her a half snort. "I don't have words. You are- absolutely breathtaking. I think I'm going to need a shield of some sort to ward off suitors from you tonight."

She doubled over with laughter. Bending at the waist, she waved off his comment until she found his gaze dropping lower. He swallowed hard. His eyes fixated on her. She lifted up, wondering what he was staring at, when she suddenly realized she had shown him a lot more than she wanted to. If what she pictured in her head was true, she had just given him a great view down her dress, including a, peek at her red-colored lacy bra, which was, presently, hidden beneath the deep V cut of her dress. She shied away, slightly embarrassed by her tawdry display. In her excitement, she, apparently, had lost all sense of decorum. She wanted to apologize to Gabe, but she didn't want to bring attention to the recent, bawdy X-rated show he'd been forced to attend.

He adjusted the seat of his pants and cleared his throat once again. He choked over his words. "Are you ready to go?"

She nodded, taking the arm he offered. He stopped just inside the door and turned to her. Running several of his fingers through her hair, he smiled. "You truly are gorgeous. I'll be your bodyguard if you want me to be."

"Thank you." She grabbed ahold of his upper arm and gazed up at him fondly. His smile slowly disappeared. He blinked his eyes and then returned his attention to the doorknob. Opening then closing the door behind them, he waited for her to lock the door before they walked out to his truck, awaiting them in the parking lot.

CHAPTER 8

GABRIEL

Marnie didn't want him to attend the Christmas party with Arabelle. When he first asked her what she thought, she said no. He wore her down over two solid days, finally telling her he was going to go whether she liked it or not. Arabelle was his best friend. He had promised her at the start of the year they'd go together. Gabe was a man of his word, and if keeping it meant losing Marnie, so be it. Almost three weeks without the joy of Arabelle's company proved almost unbearable. Definitely not something Gabe figured he'd ever experience. He found himself, at times, questioning if taking Marnie back was the right decision.

The night he went over to Marnie's for an "emergency" wasn't what he expected. She answered the door in little more than a G-string and pasties. Gabe's libido was already kicked into high gear with Arabelle. When Marnie pulled him into her home, dropped his pants and boxers, he was on the verge of telling her no. Yet, when she surrounded him with her mouth, he groaned and rolled his eyes into the back of his head. When she proceeded to bob her head up and down, sucking him, slowly at first, and then moving faster in a dizzying rhythm that had his heartbeats ready to burst out of him, he was a goner. The only thing he could do was stand still and observe her as she gave him ultimate pleasure. He only wished it was Arabelle's lips surrounding him instead of Marnie's. Yet, he was loathed to stop Marnie in her efforts, for he was so close. She kept it up until he blew his load into her mouth. One thing Marnie was always good at was jacking him. She swallowed down every last drop of his cum. Her mouth working on him, absorbing everything he had to give kept his orgasm rippling through him.

He was just about to protest and run back to Arabelle when she lay down on the carpet and spread her legs. He had to reciprocate. Besides, hearing Marnie's screams always gave him pleasure, too. By the time she was done, he was ready for his round two, and she gave it to him.

He lifted her against a wall and took her fast and hard. It was one satisfying night. It was also the start of a second chance he wasn't sure if he wanted.

Now that he was accompanying Arabelle to her party, he contemplated, again, if he had made the right decision. When she walked out into the living room, he stared at her, completely stunned. He'd never seen anything so sexy in his life. She was absolutely gorgeous, and the best part was she was beautiful inside, too. She was the ultimate woman. He could kick himself. He had a chance with her, and he blew it by running back to his ex.

Then she bent over and laughed. Immediately, his eyes dropped to the delicious view she afforded him straight down her chest. My god, the woman was incredible! She showed him the lacy edges of her red bra and didn't seem to know it. The things he envisioned doing with that body had sinful images popping into his head and tenting his pants so hard he feared she'd find the evidence of his desire before he had a chance to hide it. Shifting in his seat did very little to cover the desire he felt for her. If they weren't going to a party and he was single- If she only knew the ideas swimming about in his head. He wanted to try every one of them with her.

All he wanted was a little taste, a nibble. Yet, he knew once with Arabelle wouldn't be enough. If Arabelle gave herself to him... He closed his eyes and gritted his teeth. They were at the party, and he had to keep his composure. He searched his immediate area. There were a couple of dark places in the back of the grand ballroom they could explore- No, Gabe. Don't go there.

Arabelle thrust her feminine hand in between them. "Want to dance?"

"I thought I was supposed to ask that."

"Well, you didn't, so I am," she teased. He loved the way they bantered with each other. He slipped her hand into his and led her onto the dance floor, twirling her as soon as they stepped onto it and relishing her girlish laughter.

He smiled broadly as the song soon changed to a slow one. Taking advantage of the situation, he pulled her into him. His hands slipped to her waist, his fingers landing at the top edge of her juicy bottom. He lowered his hands to caress her heavenly globes, sighing as he stroked over each one. He then eyed her as she pulled his hands back to her waist.

"I'm not sure Marnie would like the way you're touching me right now."

"I'm not sure if I care what Marnie

thinks."

"But she's your girlfriend."

He pressed the side of his head next to hers and murmured. "You're the one I care about."

She tried shoving him away. The action only made him tighten his hold on her. "Gabe, we can't do this."

"I love you, Arabelle."

"Of course, you do. I love you, too."

"No. I *love* you. I've always loved you. I just didn't know it till now."

She slipped out of his arms and walked away. He stormed after her. Catching up to her, he placed a hand on her shoulder and swiveled her toward him. He then leaned in. She slapped him. Then she took off shortly after a few onlookers gasped at her behavior.

Gabe placed his hand over the searing spot she left on his cheek, now radiating heat. He warded off the questions and the false concern of the guests and stalked after her. After all, he put her through; he deserved the slap to his face. Yet, she had to let him explain. She had to give him a chance to somehow rectify the situation. That's all he seemed to be doing nowadays- appeasing people and putting things right. Yet, Arabelle was different. Her opinion mattered most. If she was sore with him, he'd make it right. He had to regain her trust.

He found her just outside of the hotel doors. She moved once she spotted him. He called out her name, repeating it as she moved faster away. She yelled at him and then broke out into a run. He followed, knowing full well she was no track star, and he'd catch up to her in no time. Besides, she was in heels. She was never fast in sneakers, much less heels. When she fell over, landing mostly onto the grass, he cried out her name. He fell onto his knees as soon as he was by her side. Reaching out to grab her shoulders, she kicked at him and screamed.

"Arabelle, please stop. Are you hurt?"

"Get away from me!"

"Stop. Stop, Arabelle." He turned his body to one side, thwarting her attempts to hurt him. Although she wasn't physically damaging him, her dislike of him carved bloodied, painful slices of rejection straight through his heart.

Several of her co-workers surrounded him. They pulled him off her and shoved him away. He growled at them in warning as he attempted to return to her side.

"Is this man bothering you?" one asked her while giving Gabe the stink eye.

Another shouted at Gabe. "Hey man, why don't you go away? She doesn't want you around."

"Arabelle, are you okay?" A handsome man in a grey suit hovered over her. Gabe roared. He fisted his hands and broke free of the men holding onto him.

He snarled and grabbed ahold of the grey-suit guy before shoving him away from Arabelle's side. The guy lost his footing and fell. "Stay away from her! She's mine!"

"Gabe! Stop it. You have no right."

Breathing in-out-in-out, Gabe struggled to regulate his haphazard breaths. He threw his hands out to his sides in a sign of defeat. "You want to be with him?" He pointed at the grey-suit guy, lifting up from the ground. "You'd rather his company than mine? Fine!"

She shook her head. "It's not that. It's just that you're acting like an animal right now."

He forced his words through gritted teeth. "What if I am, Arabelle? What if that's what I truly am?"

"What are you saying? Are you drunk or something? I've never seen you act this way before. I think you should go home, Gabe. Back to Marnie." She shook her head. "I'm sorry I- I'm sorry I called you. I shouldn't have. I'll find my own way home."

His heart jolted. She didn't want him around. Yet, they'd been apart for more than two weeks. He massaged the burning sensation in his chest, attempting to assuage the enormous pain throbbing through his veins.

"No. Arabelle. You need me."

The confused look she gave him sliced daggers through his soul. "Right now, Marnie needs you."

His heart shattered. He dropped his head and clutched at his chest. If he, too, dropped on the floor, he wouldn't care right now. All he wanted was Arabelle. He realized that now. He lifted his gaze and stared into her eyes which spoke more than words could say. A mixture of sadness and pity rolled into them, arousing a darker emotion within Gabe.

The men wrapped their hands around his forearms to restrain him. He threw his arms up in the air and shoved them off him before his beast rose to the surface and took care of them. "Fine. Have it your way. I'm leaving."

She scampered after him. He stopped in his tracks when she called his name.

He lowered his head when she cupped the side of his face. "Please, Gabe, don't be mad at me. Maybe we shouldn't have done this tonight. Maybe Marnie's right. I'm not good for you. I don't want to interfere with your relationship in any way. I know you're working hard on it."

He shook his head and muttered the word *no* several times. "She didn't want me to come. I did, anyway."

Arabelle removed her hand. "I didn't

know she didn't want you here tonight. You didn't tell me. You shouldn't have come."

"Why wouldn't I? It was my decision."

Her voice softened. "Gabe..."

"Apparently, I can't have what I want. It's okay. I'm leaving now."

She reached out to him. "Wait. What do you mean? Gabe, please, don't leave like this."

Placing one foot in front of the other, Gabe ignored Arabelle and pressed forward. Raising his legs to move was akin to moving boulders, yet Gabe wasn't stopping. He should've known. Arabelle didn't want him. Granted, he was still with Marnie, yet he'd been reconsidering his decision in the past week. Now he knew what he wanted. As soon as he got back home, he'd make arrangements to meet Marnie tomorrow. It was time their relationship came to a permanent end. This time, however, he'd break up with her in a public place- perhaps a park. The last thing he'd do is duplicate his error from last time. He was never setting foot in her home again.

***

When Arabelle came calling, Gabe couldn't say no. She was his weakness. As much as he wanted to avoid her, she was stubborn, much like him. She wouldn't take no for an answer, and, eventually, she showed up at his pizza shop.

As soon as she walked in, he rushed her out the door. "Arabelle, I'm working."

"I just wanted to tell you I'm sorry."

"For what?"

She caressed her hand over his left cheek. "For slapping you last night. Are you okay? It was with my left hand, and you know that one's not very strong, but still, I didn't mean to hurt you, Gabe, if I did."

He chuckled. "I'm okay. I guess I made a mess of last night, myself. I'm sorry, too."

"Can we make up for it? Say at my place. If that's okay with Marnie, that is. I don't want to interfere, but I really miss you, Gabe. You're my best friend, and I never thought we'd be separated like this."

"We're not. I'm breaking up with Marnie later today."

She drew her eyebrows together. "Oh? Okay. Are you sure?"

"She's not right for me. I knew all along, yet I chose to ignore it."

She tilted her head to one side. "How are you really doing?"

He smirked. "You know me too well. I'm okay, Arabelle. I should never have taken her back." He stroked his hand down the side of her right cheek. "She doesn't understand us. We have a special relationship. No one can break that apart."

She chewed on her lower lip. "Are we-are we okay, then?"

The start of a smile spread across his lips. "Of course."

She gave him a hug. "I've missed you, Gabe, so much. I just want this to be your decision, no one else's. I'm here if you need me."

He winked. "Don't worry. I'll call you. In the meantime, do you want lunch? I'll make your favorites."

She gave him a flirty smile. "A Sicilian pie and breadsticks? You're on!"

His heart thumped at her girlish ways. He loved her antics and never got enough of them. They did something to his insides and zapped a sure-fire pleasure signal straight to his groin. Yet, for now, he had to, somehow, ignore his attraction to her. Landing a hard slap to her bottom, he sported a mischievous grin as she skirted by him. She screeched and hollered out his name before coming to a sudden stop. Then she gave him a look before holding the front door open. He laughed aloud. It was great having Arabelle back in his life. He never should've let Marnie come between them in the first place.

After lunch, he walked her to her car, carrying an armload of extra food he made for her to take with her. She knew each time she ventured to his pizza shop; she was never going home empty-handed. He wasn't going to let his girl starve. Besides, she had sensuous curves he loved, and ingesting only bread and water wasn't going to cut it. As long as they remained friends, he was going to make sure she was taken care of. His inner beast demanded it.

He placed her food containers into the back seat. Before she slipped into the driver's seat, he grabbed ahold of her waist and closed the gap between them. Placing his forehead against hers, he inhaled her musky scent for several long seconds and then rumbled a happy sigh. He murmured into her ear.

"I'll call you later, okay?"

"If you want to. You know I'm here for you, whenever. I just worry about how you'll feel after breaking up with Marnie. If you need time, it's okay."

He closed his eyes and chuckled. Instead of going about her business, she worried about him. She was ready to give him time to process and to heal. Time he didn't need. His husky tone of voice caressed her earlobe. "Now you know why I love you." Hovering over her tempting mouth, his warm breath teased her pink lips. He considered kissing her, exactly, where he wanted to or going for her cheek, instead. Then he recalled last night's fiasco, which brought out her fiery temper. Arabelle was positively adorable when she was mad. The urge to kiss her on her lips, rousing up her anger again, had his inner beast alert, ready, and standing at attention. Yet, he was at his place of work. Drama in the parking lot wouldn't speak too highly of his establishment. He decided on the latter, giving her a soft, slow peck on her left cheek before letting her go.

He grumbled in dissatisfaction as she stepped into the driver's seat. The instant void of her soft body left a chilly emptiness he rarely experienced except in her presence. He waved at her as she sped away, regretting her absence yet satisfied that he'd see her again, soon.

Several hours later, he scrubbed a hand across his bearded chin, slipped the phone out of his front pocket, and called her.

His heart skipped a beat as soon as her lovely voice came on.

"It's done," he said. His tone of voice lowered, matching his current mood. Breaking up with Marnie was tougher than he figured it would be. She wanted to do anything, everything to keep him, including doing him out in the open, in the park they met at. Yet, Gabe was firm. They weren't a good match. He gave it a second chance, and it didn't work out. He wanted to part as friends. Marnie picked up her purse and left. So much for friendship.

"Are you okay? Is there anything I can do?"

He leaned forward on the bench, resting his weight on his elbows atop his knees. "I need you. Can you come over? I'll make dinner."

"No. I'll bring take out. You just rest. I'll be there in a few."

"Take your time. I'm still at the park."

"Oh. You want me to meet you there, instead?"

"No. Give me thirty minutes, and then come over." He wanted her in his house not wandering around a park searching for him. He pictured Arabelle's soft, kissable lips, her gorgeous, chocolate, brown eyes, and her silky brown locks and let the pleasurable sensations jolting his body into awareness wash over him. He needed Arabelle. He needed her now, nestled within his strong arms.

"Thank you," he said after receiving her agreement. He ended the call, stood up, and inhaled deeply. His nostrils picked up on all sorts of scents: crisp grass, aging tree bark, and then trash and dog poop. He wrinkled his nose and huffed as he made his way to his truck. The park was definitely nothing like the glorious woods behind his home.

CHAPTER 9

ARABELLE

Arabelle gasped as the front door swung in seconds before the chiming sound ended. She had just pressed the doorbell. She didn't expect Gabe to already be at the entrance. She smiled, stretching the corners of her lips to match Gabe's Cheshire cat-like grin.

"Hiya Belly," he said. She thrust the wrapped present into his hands. "I didn't think we were exchanging gifts yet?"

"Well, it's almost Christmas, and I figured you needed something cheerful, so I brought your gift a little sooner than expected."

"Cool," he said. Her heart stuttered as he lowered his face to hers. He gave her an affectionate peck on the cheek and lifted back up. Shutting the door behind them, he quickly made his way over to a tall, brightly decorated Christmas tree next to the fireplace. She followed him, admiring the decorations and pointing out several that were collected either individually or from their combined adventures as they explored through several states. One of the things they loved doing together was traveling. Whenever she and Gabe had the chance to get away, they would. It was a major factor in why they were best friends. Plus, he was great company and fun to be with.

She slipped off her gloves and held her hands out in front of the crackling fire as he arranged the gifts she brought under the tree. Murmuring in delight, she wiggled her fingers and closed her eyes at the welcoming warmth. Then she flipped her eyes open and gasped. "Oh, I almost forgot." Unhooking the white plastic bag from her right arm, she handed it to him. "Here's dinner. Can you place it on the counter? I'll gather the plates and utensils right after I warm up."

Closing her eyes once more, she heard him shuffling toward the kitchen. She felt the warmth from his body; surround her back when he returned. His arms snaked around her waist, and his head rested on her shoulder. Something soft caressed her cheek and jingled by her ear. She giggled. Opening her eyes with a smile, she reached up to touch the familiar red, felt hat. Her hands smoothed over the material that ended with a gold-colored bell hanging from the tip.

"So, you're Santa now?"

He winked. "Have you been naughty?"

"Not nice?" She laughed and pulled him closer, nestling into his strong arms with a wide grin. An overwhelming sense of joy warmed through her heart. She thrilled at his comforting hugs.

"I always love when you do that. Hug me from behind, that is. I've really missed this."

He squeezed her waist. "So have I."

"Shall we eat?"

"In a minute. I want to enjoy this moment with you."

She laid her head back against his shoulder, flicked the tips of her fingers across his bell, and caught the mischief in his eyes. Maybe it was his comforting warmth. Maybe it was the look in his eye that begged her for more. Whatever it was, she dropped her guard and did the unexpected. She tipped her head up toward him and let her heart take over.

Gabe leaned forward and closed his eyes. Placing her lips across his, she moaned in agreement with his guttural groan. He tightened his hold on her and coaxed her mouth to open. She met his tongue, dueling with it and teasing him. Nibbling on his lower then upper lip, she delighted in the random sounds of pleasure coming from him, as sparks of pure bliss shot through her core, spiraling down to the one area Gabe never had access to before. What started out as a simple urge to shower him with love and affection turned quickly into something more.

Gabe surprised her and took charge. Lifting her up into his arms with little effort, she squealed with half delight and half fear as he marched them toward his bedroom. With each step he took, the bell sounded, reminding her they were either making a beautiful step forward in their relationship or a huge, irreparable mistake.

"Wait. Should we be doing this? You just broke up with Marnie. Are you sure?"

He laid her gently on the bed and hovered over her. He stroked his index finger beneath her chin, tilting it up to meet his eyes. "Arabelle, I've wanted this for a long time now. Do you feel the same way? Do you want me, too?"

"Yes, Gabe. I've loved you ever since childhood, but...you didn't feel the same way." She shied away with the embarrassment, recalling how he reacted the one time she opened up to him. She swore she'd never let him in again- not in that way.

He cupped his fingers under her chin

and gently brought her back. Gazing into her eyes, he placed his index finger across her mouth. "I do now. It just took a little time apart to make me realize it." He leaned over and kissed her neck, slowly descending lower and planting a trail of kisses down her left arm. "I love you, Arabelle. I've always loved you."

She stroked her fingers through his thick hair. "I love you too, Gabe." He gently guided her back down to the bed when she tried to lift up.

"No, beautiful. It's your turn to feel pleasure. I'm going to take my time." He winked.

"But, what about dinner?" she teased.

His gruff tone of voice sent a shot of thrill straight through her body. "We're having dessert, first." She shivered with delight. He helped her out of her clothes, taking extra time nibbling the top of her breasts before he undid the hooks of her bra. Her breathing turned shallow quickly, and her eyes lowered to half-mast. She ran her fingers through his hair and murmured in his ear. "Oh god, Gabe, I've wanted you for so long. My panty is wet."

He jerked up, showering her with a mischievous grin. "Good. That's how I want you." She stroked over his hard manhood protruding from his jeans. When he paused in his attention to her to undo his zipper, she stopped him.

"No. Let me." He helped her with the button, undoing it, and then watched her take her time unzipping him. Shoving his jeans down, she rolled down his boxers and gasped. "Lord, Gabe, you kept this from me?"

He threw his head back and groaned when her hand surrounded him. He hissed when she replaced her hands with her mouth. Lord, he was large! She'd take her time to enjoy every inch of him. The sharp jingle of his bell shot an uncommon thrill through her, reminding her how affected Gabe was by what she did to him. He wanted her. At this moment, she held power over him. It was a sexy feeling- one she encountered with previous lovers. Yet, with Gabe, her best friend and the one man she admired the most, the sensation was intensified. Maybe it was because he was off-limits before, or maybe it was the fact that what they were doing seemed part taboo.

She lowered her mouth over him, taking as much of him in as possible before she rose back up. Gazing up at him, a part of her sought his reaction while a basic, primal part of her delighted in the power she held over him. Instead of pining for Gabe, like she did all those years, the tables were turned. He now wanted her.

Licking the rim of his thick, hard cock, she opened her mouth and bobbed up and down, eying him in between her strokes. His eyelashes lowered, and his eyes fixated on her as she continued the smooth up and down strokes that led to his completion. He breathed her name in between sharp jingles from the bell on his hat. The tone of his voice lowered and softened the longer she worked him. His breathing soon turned to mere puffs. His inhales became wheezy. He groaned, cursed aloud, and said her name repeatedly, his voice escalating in tone as she sped up.

Suddenly, her eyes widened when he shoved her off him. Instinctively, she swung her arms behind her, her hands taking the brunt of her weight as her bare bottom landed on the wooden floor. Gazing up at him, she wondered why he stopped her before she had the chance to delight in his release. She swiped a hand over her mouth, wiping off the remnants of his pre-cum. Maybe she wasn't good enough? Maybe he'd had better. Having had a hell of a lot more lovers than her, he was the more experienced one. She waited for his response, ready to throw her clothes back on and go home if he didn't want her. Lowering his head, he strove to catch his breath. Then he spoke. "No. I want to come inside you. If you'll let me."

She stared at him, unable to speak. What did he mean? Her eyebrows drew together, and her head tilted slightly to one side. She waited for him to explain.

"I'm clean. I know you take the pill. I want all of you, Arabelle. All- of- you." His nostrils flared. "I've never had sex without a condom before, but with you, I want to. Will you let me?"

Gabe truly wanted her. Wow. It was still a concept she had trouble wrapping her head around. She gave him a shy smile.

He reached behind him and pulled up his shirt, throwing it off to one side of the room with the Santa hat.

"No!" she shouted, reaching one arm out toward him. "Put it back on."

His eyebrows tilted into a V. "The shirt?"

"No. The hat, silly. I want to hear it jingle."

He stepped out of his jeans, pooled around his legs, and retrieved the hat. Placing it back on his head, he gave her a playful grin. "That's my girl."

He stripped the socks off him and then came for her. "Now. It's your turn." He knelt on the floor, his eyes on her the entire time as she opened her legs and, slowly, lay back. Positioning himself in front of her, he parted her thighs further open with a toothy grin. Locking his gaze with hers, she felt the impact of his words rumbling through her core. "I'm going to enjoy this." She watched him. A part of her remained in disbelief as he lowered his head between her legs.

The first stroke of his tongue across her clit almost undid her. She tried to grab ahold of something, anything, but all she felt underneath her was smooth wood. Instead, she slipped her hand beneath the bed sheet, grabbed onto the small bit of rope sewn into the mattress, making it easier to turn it over, and held on for mercy. Her eyelashes fluttered with every stroke he gave her. She could've sworn her eyes rolled to the back of her head as he continued his adoration. Attempting to cover all possible pleasure zones, he licked her slowly and thoroughly. The jingling sound of his bell lulled her straight into a pleasure-filled fantasy world. The simple sound soon turned erotic, accompanying every escalated, ragged breath she took and every jolt of pure ecstasy he gave her. Her breath squeaked as she tried to swallow in more oxygen and her heartbeats turned erratic, its steady rhythm long lost to Gabe's sexual prowess. She moaned his name repeatedly, taking long, deep inhales between each attempt. Reaching out to him, she pulled and tugged, gently, at his hair slipping out from beneath the hat as he showered her with the most amazing, sensual experience she ever had in her life. Jingle-jangle-jingle-jangle. He continued his exploration, feasting skillfully upon her, teasing, and tormenting her to a heightened zone of pleasure she'd never known. Now that she experienced Gabe, she doubted she'd ever go back. Gabe was all she ever wanted.

She sensed her body almost at the pinnacle. The slow, torturous swirls of his delicious tongue would soon mark the end of her. At least she'd die happy with a huge smile plastered across her face.

He stopped, lifted up to gaze at her, and then growled out one word before he delved back down between her thighs. "Mine."

Her pleasure rose within her, sending her up the infamous mountain of ecstasy. Climbing further and further up, she shifted her hips to give him better access till she reached the top, and then she stilled. Suddenly she shouted aloud as her safety harness broke seconds before she floated down, blissfully happy, on a fluffy, white cloud. Her body shook in the aftermath. She opened her eyes to find Gabe's one-sided grin.

"Good?" he teased. She pursed her lips and narrowed her eyelids to his low chuckle. He planted his lips on her and kissed her. Melting into him, she returned each kiss with a renewed vigor stemming straight from her heart. He pulled her into his arms and stood up. She tightened her arms around his neck, afraid she'd fall. Yet his strong arms held her thighs up. She locked her ankles together behind his back. No man had ever had sex with her in this position before. She wasn't a little thing.

Her chest against his, she held her breath as she felt him at her entrance. Gabe was serious. She'd seen this position in Kama Sutra books and even in one X-rated film before, but she never thought it would happen to her. Planting a scorching hot path of kisses across her shoulder, he whispered, "I love you," brief seconds before he plunged into her. She uttered a weak sound as he filled her to capacity, catching his slow sigh before it completely disappeared.

He murmured as he kissed her across her cheek, aiming his ardor toward her lips. "The perfect fit." Then he engaged her mouth in several long, languorous, satisfying kisses as he bobbed her up and down his long shaft. "I should've known it was you. It's always been you." Tears erupted to the surface as his words touched her heart. The way Gabe loved her, cared about her, and wanted the best for her warmed her through. He wasn't only her best friend. He was the best thing that ever happened to her. She was lucky to have found such a wonderful man. She'd never let him go.

Arabelle snuck a quick peek at Gabe. The way his muscles worked to keep her body in the air, supporting her with only his large hands beneath her thighs, was marvelous. She moved with him, lifting up then down. The feel of him inside her was indescribable. Yet, the most amazing part was that her feet weren't anywhere near the floor.

As a curvy girl, Arabelle never considered it possible. To be lifted up and draped around a man's waist so quickly and with little effort must've been a feat worthy of Hercules or maybe another Greek God found only in mythology. Yet, here she was bouncing over Gabe in the most delicious ways. In fact, all she had to do was keep her balance. He took care of everything else.

Squeezing her thighs against his sides and digging her heels into the small of his back, she kept a death grip of her interlocked arms around his neck so she wouldn't tumble to the floor.

Gabe's gruff voice beckoned her. "Look at me."

All this time, Arabelle had shied away, keenly aware she was making love to her best friend- the one man, off-limits to her, for too many years. Yet now, he wanted eye contact. She struggled to comply with his request though a part of her preferred to remain hidden.

Her gaze met his lustful irises. She scanned his handsome face, spotting the beads of sweat across his forehead and the squiggly lines of tension sporadically popping up as he tensed and relaxed. He hissed as her nipples grazed across his chest.

"Damn, you're sexy," he growled. He brushed his lips across her neck, planting a short line of kisses directly beneath her earlobe and down. He groaned when she whimpered. Then he maneuvered them over to the bed and gently laid her down on it as if she were fine treasured porcelain.

He clambered onto the bed and hovered over her just long enough to taste her lips before he flipped them over. Straddling his thighs, she gave him a questioning look. He only smiled at her. Uncomfortable with the change of position, she attempted to move off him when he locked his hands behind her knees.

"No. I want to see you. Beautiful you."

He flattered her. Still, she knew she had too many curves to fit the ideal.

Before she had the chance to protest,

he lifted his arms, cupping each of her breasts in the palms of his hands. He closed his eyes and groaned as his fingers traced over her soft, tender skin and rubbed across her nipples, turning them into tight peaks. She felt him lingering at her entrance. His hands grabbed at her waist, tugging at her and urging her down.

"My god, Arabelle, don't make me wait any longer."

She moaned as she slid over his fascinating length. Gabe was truly well endowed. She'd never had such an amazing experience with any of her lovers. He started up his rhythm again, the bell on his hat jingling with every effort he made. Then he quickened his pace. Placing one hand on the back of the headboard, he lifted up to give himself leverage while remaining within her. He then did something she had never considered. He reached for her, brought her hand straight to his lips, and then kissed it. Next, he slipped her hand within his and gently squeezed it while he gave her a wide, cheerful grin. He moved within her, slowing down at times and then moving faster, all while keeping ahold of her hand. Her long moans intertwined with his guttural groans. Their sounds escalated as he grew closer. His strokes becoming almost feverish, she felt him growing impossibly larger. His hat, tilting off to one side, threatened to fall off his head. All of a sudden, he stilled. Throwing his head back, the hat fell off him. The ringing sound carried through the air and crashed to the floor, bouncing once then twice as he shouted out his pleasure. Warm liquid jetted into her. He lowered his head and sighed out her name before collapsing back onto the bed, releasing her hand in the process. She shifted off to one side of him. Her head nestled into an adjacent pillow. Grabbing ahold of her, Gabe pulled her straight into his arms and softly kissed her.

"I love you, Arabelle. You're mine. Say you're mine."

She squeezed her arms around him. "I am, Gabe. I love you, too. So very much."

"I'm so happy, Arabelle. You make me happy."

She tilted her head to one side and, gingerly, swept a hand through his hair. "That's all I want for you. I want you to be happy."

He snuck a kiss. "Mine. Mine, always."

She teased. "Not unless I find someone else."

He tilted her chin up to look at him. His eyes shifted side to side, searching for something within hers. "What? Dean? Oh." He chuckled. "You're not serious. Good. There are no other guys, Arabelle. There never will be. Don't you know that by now?"

She snuggled into his arms and smiled. Resting her head against his chest, she heard his heartbeat. The rhythm soothed her and lulled her. She closed her eyes.

He gently shook her. "Hey. Hey. Don't fall asleep now. We need to eat. That was just dessert."

She laughed. "I guess you're hungry, then?'

His gaze raked over her nude form. "I'm always hungry."

She, playfully, tapped him on the nose. "No more dessert until we eat dinner. I'm sure it's cold by now."

He nuzzled her neck and murmured. "That's okay. I know how to warm things up."

She kissed his cheek. "I can't argue with that."

CHAPTER 10

ARABELLE

Arabelle wasn't sure what to think. She stared at the phone in her hand for a long while before placing it back on the charger. Marnie had just invited her to a weekend getaway in the mountains. During the short period of time Marnie had dated Gabe, she supposed she and Marnie had become more than acquaintances. They had even double-dated some, taking overnight trips with their guys to local destinations yet, a camping trip, alone, with Marnie? That never happened.

Still, Marnie wanted some girl time. She confided she didn't have many girlfriends. She swore she was over Gabe though she confessed on wondering how he was doing.

How was Gabe doing? Amazingly well. He was just over at Arabelle's place last night taking care of her needs. Gabe confessed, at the time, that he had never bathed with a female before. She found this odd, as he definitely had his share of women in the past. Yet, he seemed intent on engaging in waterplay with her. After pulling her into the shower, sporting a wicked grin, he explored and thoroughly mastered her body. She recalled the intense hunger in Gabe's eyes and the way he pawed at her, holding onto her and using her body for their mutual pleasure. It was the most delightful and satisfying experience of her life. Arabelle giggled, recalling the naughtiness they engaged in. Each time, with Gabe, was spectacular. She never thought she'd have a chance with him. The fact that he wanted her still puzzled her. Each time she worried if she was doing the right thing- dating her best friend- she pushed aside the fear and remembered that what they had was a two-way street. Gabe enjoyed her company, and she loved his. It was almost as if they were meant for each other. As if the stars aligned just for them.

Marnie seemed to take the news well- that she was dating Gabe. The reaction Arabelle expected, instead, resulted in strange acceptance.

"I knew you two were meant for each other. I could see it in the way he looked at you. The way he dropped everything to be with you."

"But that didn't always happen." Arabelle retorted.

"Oh yeah, it did. You were just blind to it."

Arabelle didn't think so. Still, what Marnie said was true. Gabe almost always showed up when she needed him. She considered his response a friendly gesture since they were the closest of friends. It was also sweet. It's what made Gabe reliable, unique, and, well- Gabe.

"So, do you want to go? It'll be fun. You have your gear?"

"Yeah. I still do." She pondered Marnie's question. She'd spend a weekend away from Gabe- nowhere near his impeccable, toned body, his warm smile, and his tender kisses. Did she want to go off the grid with her ex-rival, or did she want to remain cozied up in Gabe's arms, relishing all the love and passion he had to give?

"Sure. I'll go with you." Arabelle loved the outdoors, plus she was curious to find out how Marnie was doing since the breakup. A weekend away from Gabe might be fun. It would give them the chance to find out if that old saying was true. Did absence make the heart grow fonder?

"Great. I'll see you Saturday."

That's how Arabelle found herself in

the woods on a Saturday afternoon with Marnie instead of Gabe. They had just checked into their campsite and were now exploring the area. She glanced around her, taking in the breathtaking view. The air was a cool fifty degrees-chilly but not too bad for the middle of the day. The sky was crisp and cloudless. The clear blue color mimicked some of the beautiful oceans she and Gabe explored in the past. The trees, nearly empty of all their leaves, wove unspoken tales of their majestic lifespan.

Marnie, trailing a few feet behind, called out to her. "This was a good idea, right?"

Arabelle took a step and then another, checking her footing as she continued up a small hill. "Yeah, it was. Thanks for inviting me. I didn't think you wanted to talk to me since...you know. Listen, I have to be frank with you. It's kind of weird being here with you when you and Gabe aren't together anymore. I'm really sorry about that, by the way."

"Don't worry about it. It's fine. I'm dating now, and I'm having fun. Gabe's not for me. I think he was always waiting for you."

Arabelle snorted. "I don't know, but I am glad you're okay with me dating him. I wouldn't want to hurt you. You're a good person, Marnie."

"What is that saying again? Let bygones be bygones? It's in the past, Arabelle. Let's keep it there."

Arabelle nodded. "Sounds good to me. So, tell me about your dates? Anyone serious?"

"Well... There is this one." Marnie proceeded to share details about one guy she was really into. His name was Paul. From the way she described him, he seemed like the ultimate catch. Arabelle smiled as Marnie regaled stories of a few of their adventures, with one ending in steamy role-playing.

Arabelle whipped out her plastic bottle from her backpack, took a long swig, and then sputtered the contents out when Marnie added another racy detail to the story. Arabelle bent over and coughed to catch her breath. Yet, each cough led to another, creating a domino effect. She grabbed ahold of her chest while Marnie pounded the palm of her hand on her upper back.

Marnie hovered over Arabelle. "Are you okay? I'm sorry."

Arabelle lifted up, inhaled deeply, and cleared her throat. She shook her head and laughed. "Well, I guess I wasn't ready for that. So he likes anal?"

"Yeah. Crazy, huh?"

Arabelle stared at her. Her lips wouldn't form the question she desperately wanted answered. An image of Gabe bent over Marnie's back branded into her brain. His hands grabbed ahold of her hips. He rocked them back and forth to a mind-numbing rhythm as he plundered into her. Marnie struggled to catch her breath, and Gabe threw his head back and shouted her name before he came in a different hole. Did he wear a condom, or did his seed stream out of her like it did last night when she was with Gabe?

Marnie snapped her fingers in front of Arabelle's eyes. "Hey. Yoohoo. You okay? I was talking to you."

"Sorry, I-" Arabelle was at a loss for words. What could she tell her? That she imagined her and Gabe going at it in a way she never wanted to experience with Gabe?

"In case you're wondering, Gabe and I never went there."

Arabelle breathed out a sigh of relief, happy that Marnie volunteered that bit of information. Although Arabelle had no right to question Gabe's past sexual experiences, she couldn't help wondering if she measured up to the females in his past.

"So, what are you doing for Christmas?"

"Spending it with Gabe, I guess. And you?"

Marnie giggled. "I think I'm spending it with Paul."

Arabelle laughed at Marnie's quip. She couldn't help picturing exactly how they'd spend it. The only question she had was where? In the bed, on the floor, up against a wall, or maybe outside in nature, naked and under a tree? Arabelle chortled. All kidding aside, Arabelle was glad Marnie found a good man.

"I'm happy for you, Marnie. I'm glad you found someone nice who treats you well."

Marnie thumbed at the scenery behind her. "Thanks. Want to head back? I'm getting kind of hungry."

"Me too. Let's go."

Arabelle swiveled on her heel and walked for what seemed a mini eternity when she thought she heard something to her left. Jerking her head toward the sound in an attempt to find the source, she gasped and took a step back when she saw something that shouldn't be there. Marnie followed her gaze. Arabelle's lips trembled as she sputtered out a single word. "B-B-Bear!"

Marnie took off in the opposite direction, shouting over her shoulder at Arabelle as she placed more distance between her and the wild animal. "Run!"

Instead of moving, Arabelle froze. She willed her legs to move, but her traitorous stems wouldn't cooperate. Instead, they were locked in place with her unwavering gaze. She'd be lunchmeat soon.

The bear was large. Apparently, it ate well, for its solid, black-colored fur was impeccable. Her eyes grazed over its features, awed with its beautiful color shimmering in the waning sunlight. One look at its wild features should've had her sprinting for her life. Instead, her curiosity peaked along with a crazy appreciation for its beauty. Its gentle, black eyes landed on hers. The color was sharp and rich, like the black obsidian stone she found one day in a shop and bought. She found herself mesmerized, languishing within the deep pools of its irises.

"Arabelle!" Marnie yelled. Still, Arabelle didn't follow her friend. Although she'd never be able to explain it, somehow, she knew this great beast meant her no harm. It was mostly gentle and, only, merely curious at her presence. Marnie shouted her name again, frantically trying to get her attention when Arabelle did the unthinkable. She knelt on the ground and called to the bear-like an owner calling out to their dog.

"Come here," she said, a part of her wondering what in the hell she was doing and how fast the bear would maul her to pieces for her lack of common sense. It would swiftly and easily end her life before it truly began. What would she miss the most? Gabe. An image of his handsome face popped into her head. His parted lips mouthed her name as his husky tone of voice called it. She'd also miss Junebug and Whiptail. Who'd take care of them once she was gone? Gabe? Every time he took them out, maybe he'd think of her, too?

I love you, Gabe. I guess we'll never know what we could've been. I'm sorry. I just know this bear won't harm me. I have to take a chance.

Still, she trembled as the bear took short strides toward her, closing the distance between them. Trudging through dense, fallen leaves, its large, furry paws stamped the ground with every lumbering step it took. Her heartbeats escalated, and her thoughts turned erratic. Maybe she should run. Maybe she should go while she still had a reasonable chance. When it was mere feet in front of her, it stopped. She swallowed down a sudden dry lump forming in the back of her throat. She stared at the bear and waited, contemplating what its next move would be. Was the bear a he or a she? She had no idea about these things, and she, certainly, wasn't going to try to examine the bear now to figure out how to address it.

Arabelle swiveled her head to her right when she heard something crunching across dead leaves approaching her. She stared at Marnie, wide-eyed. "What are you doing? Go back to the cabin."

Marnie shifted off to one side and hid most of her behind a thick tree trunk. "What are you doing? This is dangerous."

"I don't know. I think it's safe. It's crazy, I know. I'd never do this, normally, but I don't think it will harm me."

Marnie screeched. "It's a friggin' bear! My god, Arabelle, your love of animals is going to kill you."

"Let's hope not today." Arabelle turned toward the bear that was now lying on the forest floor. Its eyes zeroed in on her. His body lay in a pose like that of the famous Egyptian sphinx statue. His paws almost interlocked, looked as if he was set to pray to a higher power- an action Arabelle likely needed to consider, quickly, if this venture took an unexpected turn.

Arabelle muttered under her breath. "Seriously, Marnie, you don't have to be here. I don't want to put you in danger."

Marnie crossed her arms in front of her chest and planted her feet wide. "No. I'm not leaving you."

Arabelle wished her friend would leave. There was no use putting them both in danger when Arabelle just wanted to get a closer look at the beautiful animal. "Can you hear me, little bear? You're really beautiful."

The animal chuffed. Then she heard words directed to her from out of nowhere. *That's the first time I've been called little.*

Her eyes shifted left, then right, and then back at the animal. Who in the hell spoke to her? It wasn't a voice she recognized, and there was only her, Marnie, and this bear in her immediate area. Did the bear talk to her? She almost laughed, then reconsidered the maneuver with the bear's staunch attention on her. One false move, and it could attack. She didn't want it thinking she was a threat to it in any way.

Still, the question remained. Who spoke to her? Who answered for the bear? She twisted her head toward Marnie and asked the question though Marnie was, likely, too far away to hear exactly what she said to the bear. "Did you say something?" When Marnie shook her head, she, hesitantly, turned toward the animal. Her eyes widened, and her mouth gaped open. If no one spoke to her, that only meant one thing. She, seriously, needed to reconsider leaving. Maybe there was room behind Marnie's tree? Could she sprint there in enough time? The only other theory was that she had lost all her marbles. That was always a possibility, especially since she started a relationship with the one man she never thought would ever consider her. There was no way this bear talked to her.

Please don't be scared. I know you're wondering who's talking to you. It's me. The black bear in front of you.

She squealed, leapt up from her crouched position, and ran in Marnie's direction, shouting all the way. With Marnie close behind, following her, she made tracks for where- she had no freaking clue. All she knew was she had to get the hell out of there, away from the killer beast talking to her.

She soon heard a loud thumping sound behind her and even heavier breathing. She didn't dare to look back. If the thing was going to kill her, so be it. She'd give it some good exercise before it tackled her down. She considered climbing up a tree until she remembered she didn't know how to climb them. Besides, didn't black bears climb trees? She'd be a buffet waiting for the bear up there. A sharp pain tinged her sides as she heaved her scant breaths in and out, pumping her arms back and forth with her best effort. She wasn't a marathon runner. Her muscles were achy, her lungs burned, and she was lost and, likely, nowhere near the cabin. What in the world was she going to do now?

Arabelle.

Her right knee almost gave out, and she cursed. Who called her name? Was it Marnie? She glanced back, quickly, to find Marnie tearing off at high speed, swiftly surpassing her. Apparently, Marnie didn't call her name. When Marnie was miles ahead of her, she heard her name again.

Arabelle.

She stumbled over something and fell atop a mish-mashed pile of smelly leaves. Holy shit! She was going to die. All because a damn rock, tree branch, or a bunch of slippery leaves got in her way. It was just like one of those horror movies. There was no way in hell she was waiting to be killed. She tried scampering up, but the bear moved closer. He was almost upon her when she lifted up from the ground.

She squirmed back, thrusting all her weight on her little legs and pushing off them, hard, to get away. "Please." She didn't stop. Rolling her butt across mud, dirt, and grime, she hoped the action would aid her in slipping further away from the bear stalking her.

"Please, don't hurt me," she shouted

as a last-ditch effort, hoping beyond hope that if the bear was the one speaking to her, he'd have some sense of mercy and find his next meal somewhere else. She doubted she'd taste as good as...as...wait a minute. What did black bears eat, anyway? Weren't they, mostly, vegetarians?

The bear staggered to a stop, tousled its head, and snorted. Shaking its head back and forth, it made light chuffing sounds, almost as if it were human, in the middle of a fit of giggles. It then bobbed its head up and down. It continued making low, growly noises and then abruptly stopped. Instead of taking advantage of the situation and booking it, Arabelle stared at it with a mixture of confused amusement. She looked over to her right. Maybe there was still time to get away? The muscles in her body gave her a sharp rebuttal. She grimaced with the leftover spasms weaving through her thighs.

I'm not going to hurt you. I'd never hurt you, Arabelle.

"You are talking to me. But...how? You're an animal."

We have a connection.

"I'm human. You're an animal."

Sometimes, I can be. Its mouth curled up at each corner. She could've sworn the beast grinned. Wow. She really was losing it. What would Gabe say right now?

I am Gabe.

She snorted. The beast didn't flinch. She stared at it for a few seconds and then doubled over with laughter.

She pointed at the bear. "No, you're not."

Yes.

"No."

Yes. We can do this all day. Do you really want this?

"Prove it."

The bear collapsed into a seated position. His form soon changed. Large paws shrunk into human hands. Claws retracted into nails, and the fur across his skin transformed into lighter-colored, human skin. Arabelle's jaw gaped open the entire time the bear morphed into a more familiar form- one she'd grown fond of over the years. She couldn't believe what she saw.

"Gabe!" She moved closer, reaching one hand out to touch his lower arm. Then she flinched, retracting her fingers back as if a snake bit her. When nothing happened, she reached out to him, again, this time with two hands. She made contact with soft, warm skin. Her eyes widened before her gaze dropped.

"You're naked."

He smirked. "Well, yes, I don't shift with clothes on."

She scrambled up from the floor and took several steps back. The trembling in her voice betrayed her. "You don't what? What are you, Gabe?"

He reached for her. "Don't be afraid. I'm a shifter."

Just then, Arabelle's backpack swung off her shoulder. It banged to the ground but not before a pop-top container slipped out an open side. The sweet, amber liquid spilled generously, across the dirt, over individual blades of brown, dead grass, and across the top half of a rock. The contents, almost entirely, emptied out of the plastic bottle before Arabelle retrieved it and capped the top. She swiped her tongue over the gloppy sides, grimacing in disgust as she tasted bits of gravel. Gabe's eyes widened. He reached for the bottle, swiping his index finger over one last, remaining drop. Inserting the glazed sweetness into his mouth, he pushed his index finger past his teeth, closed his eyes, and sighed as he sucked on the morsel of heaven left behind. Popping open his eyelids, he grabbed ahold of Arabelle's arm. He spoke through gritted teeth. "We must go. Now!"

CHAPTER 11

ARABELLE

Arabelle tried to shake him off, but Gabe was insistent. He pulled at her while she retracted.

"Arabelle. Now!"

Yet, she stood her ground. She soon regretted her decision when she heard a thunderous roar that seemed close- too close. Snapping her neck to the right, her eyes widened, finding the unbelievable spectacle bearing down upon them. The area they were in was pretty safe and not known for wild animals- at least not any that would pose a threat. Yet, there it was. An impossibly huge brown bear coming toward her. Nothing stood in its way except for Gabe. He quickly fell onto all fours and stepped in front of her, unafraid and, amazingly, calm.

She gazed at Gabe, awestruck, as black fur dotted his smooth skin and replaced it entirely. His white teeth elongated and widened. His feet turned into huge, padded paws with long, sharp claws hanging over the ends of them. His ears shortened and rounded, sitting perfectly atop each side of his head. From behind, Gabe almost looked cuddly. Maybe even cute. Like one of those life-sized, fluffy bears kids loved to play with and squeeze the stuffing out of. Yet, with his haunches arched and his hair standing on end, she knew Gabe wasn't preparing himself for loving caresses. He was set on protecting her.

The brown bear was larger than Gabe. Arabelle worried for his safety. What if he died? Oh, God! She couldn't put that thought out there in the universe. Not now. Not ever.

"Gabe, don't," she pleaded. Yet, he wasn't listening. She watched, helplessly, as Gabe pounded his front paws on the ground and ushered a rolling growl in warning.

She had to do something to help him. She searched her immediate area for a large stick or something to throw at the bear. Maybe a rock or several rocks, all at once, to take its attention off of Gabe, at least for the moment. The bear grew closer. Gabe stood on his hind legs and roared. Suddenly, the bear stopped in its tracks, tilted its head to one side, and regarded Gabe with a strange look of curiosity. Then it did the unexpected. Arabelle squealed as the brown bear charged at them.

Instinctively, she took several steps back and then stopped. There was no way she was leaving Gabe. Slapping her hands over her mouth, she screamed into them as the two bears lunged at each other. What could she do? She wasn't going to sit here and watch Gabe's demise. She had to do something. Grabbing at several medium to large-sized rocks, she threw them at the brown bear, shouting with glee when they hit its fur on its side. It growled loudly and took a step toward her before Gabe tore at him. The enormous size of the brown bear was certainly impressive, and it likely, made it stronger. Yet, Gabe held an advantage. His smaller stature actually made him quicker than the lumbering giant. While the brown bear was trying to gain its bearings, Gabe danced around it, throwing jabs at it, biting into its fur, and slashing at it with little to no retort from the beast.

When the brown bear swung right, Gabe shifted left and vice versa. After several minutes of the agonizing game, the brown bear rumbled its dissatisfaction and, suddenly, shoved its large paws up in the air. Slamming its massive legs down, Arabelle sucked in air as Gabe narrowly escaped demise with his quick thinking. He rushed through the bear's arms in the nick of time. If Gabe was squashed, his efforts at protecting her might've landed him in the emergency room with broken ribs or worse.

Arabelle shouted. "Gabe, stop this, please!" She quickly regretted her attempt at intervention when Gabe swung his head toward her and received a sharp blow to the left side of his face. Arabelle screamed. She started forward, wanting to help Gabe but finding the massive brown bear looming over Gabe's body.

Flinging her arms in the air, she shouted at the top of her lungs. "Get out! Get out! Go away, you stupid bear. Go!"

Gabe seemed to take advantage of the bear's attention on her. He leapt up off the ground. Yet, the way he walked, in a dizzying fashion, indicated to her he wasn't well. Gabe needed to regain his strength. She had to keep the brown bear's attention off him and on her.

Arabelle's anger rose within her. She screamed again. The brown bear lifted to a stand and regarded her with a blank look. She shouted more as it started turning its head away, trying to keep its focus on her instead of Gabe. She'd never forgive herself if she ended up the reason for Gabe's demise.

"Yeah, look at me, you big baboon! Is this what you want? Is this what you came for?" She flung the bottle of honey out in front of her, shaking it in her hands, making sure she caught the bear's full attention. Somewhere in the back of her mind, she knew what she was doing was crazy, irrational, and likely wrong. No outdoor manual in the world advised shaking a bottle of honey in front of a giant, wild animal, yet here she was, attempting to act fearless and brave when her feet urged her to run the other way and save herself. Yet, she wouldn't do it. Gabe was hurt. He needed her. She'd go down fighting if she had to. Even against an impossible, formidable opponent like the brown bear in front of her, licking its chops with relish, preparing for its next meal.

Arabelle.

She ignored the voice in her head. She wouldn't let Gabe die. If it ended up a choice between Gabe or her perishing right then and there, then by Gods, she'd take his place. Lord, help her! She knew one slash from the bear's sharp claws would render her mauled if not dead. Yet, she was the reason Gabe was in the forest, to begin with. She wouldn't go down without a fight, even if she had no chance of winning.

Arabelle. Don't do that for me.

She uncapped the top and swung the bottle in front of her, left to right, to keep the bear's attention. Drops of honey-coated the remnants of crunchy grass beneath her. She addressed Gabe. "You're hurt. I won't let him hurt you anymore." She backed away, taking several steps at a time while the brown bear slowly approached.

Gabe grunted and then roared. He growled low, raising his tone to a high pitch when the beast turned toward him. Gabe lunged. The brown bear swiped at his lustrous, black fur. Arching quickly away from him, Gabe sped toward the forest, past several trees, leaving Arabelle stunned. The brown bear shot after him. Arabelle watched as their images grew smaller in the distance and, eventually, disappeared.

Her gaze riveted to the last area she saw Gabe. She drew in several shallow, ragged breaths, keeping an eye out for him. Sending up a quick prayer for his safe return, she faintly wondered in what condition she'd find him in. Whatever was happening in the forest right now, beyond her sight, she hoped it ended victoriously for Gabe.

What in the hell was the bear doing in the forest, anyway? The campsite's surrounding areas weren't known for bears. There were no warnings of any kind posted, and she hadn't received a flyer or additional notice by any of the camp volunteers that would've warned her to be on the lookout for any. This one must've been either hungry or brave to have ventured out this far. And now Gabe was paying for it...

She swallowed back the bitter sadness slamming into her gut as several tears threatened to escape the corners of her eyes. Oh God, no. Let him be safe. Her spine straightened with the agonizing roar coming from beyond the forest. Instinctively, she ran toward the sound's origin and then stopped. Oh god. What was she doing? What would she do if she found him...dead? She halted in her haste. Taking one hesitant step forward, she took two and then three.

She shouted. "Gabe? Gabe? Are you okay? Please say you're okay. Please."

Another torturous bellow almost rendered her speechless.

"Oh god. Gabe, please. Please be okay."

After what seemed an eternity, a black nose poked out of the woods, followed by a long brown snout and beautiful, lush, black fur. The breath she, unwittingly, held in whooshed out of her. With tears in her eyes, she threw her hands up in the air and broke into a run, screaming Gabe's name. She'd never been so happy to see a bear in her entire life. She rushed toward him without another thought, stopping in her tracks when she spotted patches of blood on his fur and underneath his claws.

She pointed at him. "Oh God, Gabe. You're hurt."

It's okay. The bear won't be bothering you anymore.

She reached out to him. "You're not injured?"

Just a few scrapes, cuts, and bruises. Nothing my body can't handle. I heal pretty quickly.

Gabe lifted up, stood on two feet, and shifted back to his human form.

Her eyes widened. "Holy cow, that's amazing. You're gorgeous. In both forms." Her eyes lowered down his body and settled on the spot between his thighs. She could've sworn it swelled a little with her avid attention.

The corners of his lips curved even higher, forming into the widest smile she'd ever witnessed. "Thank you, beautiful."

He grabbed ahold of her hand and kissed the back of it. Then he led her deeper into the forest.

She pulled back. "Wait. Where are we going? You're not going to show me the bear, are you?"

"Nope. I'm taking you in the opposite direction. I need to wash up."

"Oh...uh....You're still naked."

"Are you ashamed?"

"God no, you're hot!" She widened her eyes and then slapped both hands over her mouth to stop from spilling out any more secrets.

He leaned in. Caressing his fingers gently down the left side of her face, he whispered, "So are you, gorgeous." He lowered his mouth to hers, hovering over her lips before sealing them with a kiss. Then he lifted back with a sigh of regret. "I love you, Arabelle." Squeezing her hand, he urged her to walk with him. "Come. I need to rinse off quickly. Let me show you the lake."

She tugged at his arm. "Did you kill it?"

He stopped and regarded her. "Do you really want to know?"

She mashed her lips together and considered his question. "No... Not really, I guess."

He urged her forward. "That's what I thought."

"But...why...why was it here? What did it want? Did it want my jar of honey? I heard bears have a good sense of smell."

He shook his head. "It wanted you."

She pointed at herself. "Me? Why?"

"You're in heat. Your odor is different, and it's...well..enticing to bears." Gabe's eyes narrowed. She caught his throat working down a long swallow. "He just didn't know you belonged to me, that's all."

She trembled at his suggestion that the bear wanted her. "But-but-I'm human."

Gabe shrugged his shoulders. "When you're a lonely bear... Anything is possible. He was lost. Out of his element."

She arched her eyebrows. "Are you saying that wild animals can mate with humans?"

Gabe shook his head. "Not normally. Like I said, this one was lost, lonely and hungry, too. Your smell is like a delicious dessert. It's an irresistible perfume at this time."

Her jaw dropped. She lowered her voice. "Was he a-a-shifter or a real bear?"

Gabe gave her a side grin. "Babe, I'm a real bear."

"No, that's not what I meant-"

"I know exactly what you meant. To answer your question, he was a real bear, not a shifter like me."

"That's so strange. I just can't believe he was coming after me."

Gabe tugged at her arm and led her forward. "Not anymore."

They wandered aimlessly through the slim trees. Arabelle considered the journey random, yet Gabe seemed to know exactly where he was heading. Occasionally he'd lift his head, sniff the air, and state," it's this way." She followed him until she spotted what he'd been searching for. Most of the lake had been frozen over. Still, Gabe found an area, off to one side that remained open.

"Isn't that water really cold?"

"Yeah, but it's good for cleaning and rinsing off." To prove his point, he dug his hands into the ice-cold water and swooshed puddles of water over his head and down his sides. Then he shook his body with all his might. She threw her hands up in the air and shouted his name as water droplets splashed off him and onto her. He stopped and grinned at her.

She, playfully, smacked him across one bare shoulder. "You cad. You did that on purpose."

His grin widened.

She sat next to him, on the edge of the lake. Unzipping her backpack, she lifted out a small, red and white checkered picnic blanket and gave it to him. He folded it beneath him.

"What did you say you were, again?"

"A shapeshifter. Except my primary form is what you saw."

She shook her head. "You're kidding, right. This can't be true."

"It is."

"How long have you been like this?"

"All my life."

She inhaled a sharp, shaky breath. "You've always been this way, and you never told me?"

He hung his head in reply.

"Gabe?" She looked over at him. Emotions welled up within her, whirling about her insides and slicing directly through her heart. Words failed her. They gazed at each other over long, intense seconds. "You never told me. You had this secret all along, and you never shared it with me. Don't you trust me? Didn't you want to share this side of yourself with me? Was I not good enough to know?"

Gabe swiveled toward her. He knelt in front of her and placed his hands atop her shoulders. "No! You won't take this upon yourself, and you won't degrade yourself in front of me. It has nothing to do with you. It's me. I didn't know how to tell you. I worried you'd think less of me. Over the years, I kept coming up with excuses not to tell you. I didn't want to lose you. And...I didn't want you to fear me." He turned away from her. "I'm sorry, Arabelle. I know I ruined everything by keeping this a secret from you."

"Does anyone else know?"

He shook his head.

"Your parents?"

"They had to tell me when I started having nightmares in my early teens. They knew the change was happening. They're the only ones that know."

She stumbled back. "Are they?"

He shot a hand toward her. "Please don't be scared. Please don't. That's what I feared. I don't want you ever to be scared of me. You have nothing to fear. I would never harm you, Arabelle. Never."

"I don't know, Gabe. This was a huge secret, and you kept it from me the entire time you've known me. I don't know what to think of that. It hurts." She looked over her shoulder. "Listen. Marnie might come searching for me, or maybe she called a search and rescue group by now to find me. It's not good if she sees you out here, especially naked. You need to go."

"We need to talk."

Arabelle shook her head. "Not now. Marnie's probably worried about me. I gotta head back." She looked up at Gabe, who was already standing and handing her back her picnic blanket. She retrieved it from him, stood, and shoved the blanket back into her backpack. "I want to thank you for what you did back there with the bear. I'm sorry that happened, but if it weren't for you, I might not be alive right now."

"I will always protect you, no matter what. Please... let's talk later. I can come back here or near your campsite if you like."

"No. I need to be alone. I need time to process all this and what it means."

"I'm no different, Arabelle. I'm just a bear shifter."

She quipped. "There's a lot that goes with that, Gabe."

"You don't understand. Besides my enhanced hearing, sense of smell, vision, and ability to lift more weight than any human, I'm not much different than your average man. Oh, yeah, and I can run pretty fast, too." He smirked. "I gave you a big head start back there."

"Were both of your parents.... "

"Bears. Yes."

"So, you're not a hybrid or anything, if that even exists?"

"No."

She drew in a shaky breath. "Still. I don't know. You kept this secret from me, Gabe. It really hurts. We're best friends." She huffed out a sad sigh. "I've got to go."

He rushed over to her. "Let me take you back to where we met up, originally. At least let me do that for you. You know your way to the campsite from there."

She nodded and then stared, for several long seconds, at the hand Gabe held out toward her, hesitant to accept his gesture of friendship. Her head felt like she was swimming underwater, and she was confused at the mixed emotions tugging at her heart.

"Take it, Arabelle. Please."

She glanced into his warm, brown irises, a strange mixture of yearning and regret captivating her. She swallowed back the uncommon dryness building up in the back of her throat and, finally, slipped her hand into his, watching him as he brought the back of her hand to his lips and gently kissed it. The affection she found in his sad eyes almost brought tears to her own.

"Thank you, Arabelle, for trusting me." With that, he took a step forward, and she followed. The trek back to the spot where she first met his bear was a long, arduous, silent journey. The urge to say something to Gabe, to fill the void with conversation- even a rambling, lightheaded one- had her opening and then closing her mouth several times. Yet, she couldn't get over the fact that Gabe hadn't shared, with her, what he truly was. All these years she'd known him, he'd held this grand secret from her. She didn't understand why.

Being a bear shifter was a major part of who he was. Since he held back this part of him from her, she couldn't honestly say if she knew who Gabe was. She wasn't sure what to do now. She definitely, had no idea who she made love to in his cabin. All she knew was that she was happy back then when she didn't know. And now? She felt confused and betrayed. Her heart seemed heavier now, filled to the brim, almost overflowing with sorrow.

When they finally arrived at their destination, he clasped his hand across her forearm before letting her go. "I love you, Arabelle."

She'd normally return the sentiment without hesitation. Yet, this time, she wasn't sure how to respond. Did she love Gabe? She supposed her love for him would never stop. Yet, did she want to be with him knowing what he was now? She didn't know. She also didn't want to give him any false hope or promises. Knowing he wasn't human and that he kept this gigantic part of him from her changed everything.

"Bye, Gabe." She caught the sudden sadness within his irises before she turned away. He took a step toward her as if he wanted to say or do something. Yet, he didn't stop her from walking away. She assumed he, too, was in pain. Every step she added between them likely plunged a knife deeper into his heart, as it did hers.

She sensed the serrated, sharp blade of the invisible dagger chopping at and shredding the remnants of the once solid, vibrantly alive organ that filled with love each time Gabe was near. More than anything, she wanted to turn around, run straight into his arms and reassure him this was all temporary and she'd be back. To let him know that his startling revelation had no effect on her or her decision regarding their future. Yet, she couldn't. She'd always been honest with Gabe from the start.

The urge to sneak a peek at him, determining if he was okay, begged her to take action. Still, she ignored the intense need and, instead, aimed in the direction of the cabin to find out if Marnie had returned there unharmed.

CHAPTER 12

GABRIEL

Stupid. That's what he was. Although he anticipated Arabelle's reaction to his startling revelation, he must've expected a different outcome. What did you want, in the end? He asked himself. For Arabelle to run straight into your arms and make love to you in the forest, under the bare, skeleton-like trees? Stupid. And naive. That's what he was. For expecting her to act differently and for not telling her, in the first place, what he was.

Now he remained home alone, stewing in his misery while Arabelle ventured back to her apartment days ago. He attempted to contact her, yet each of his calls went straight to voicemail. After leaving, at least ten of them, he didn't leave anymore, switching his tactics to texting instead. Yet, all of his attempts to communicate with her remained unanswered.

Gabe grunted. Arabelle was exercising her need for space. He didn't like it. Although he'd, begrudgingly, give her the time she needed, he didn't have to enjoy their separation. In fact, he hated it.

He considered showing up at her home, unannounced. Possibly with a large bouquet of red roses and a card of apology, yet he already did that. Granted, he didn't deliver the flowers to her, personally. A delivery company took care of that, plus the card he bought from their store.

The prospect of seeing Arabelle in any mood, besides her usual joyful and happy, had him bolted to his seat, unable to move. The last thing he wanted was to cause her further pain, especially with his presence. Still, he wanted to know her thoughts, her feelings, and the current status of their relationship. If only she'd give him a second chance.

When she didn't show up at his pizza shop on Monday, Tuesday, or even Wednesday, her sudden absence struck him like a samurai sword slicing straight through his broken heart. He growled long and low. Damn it. He missed her. He didn't know how much more of her silence he could take. Already, his beast longed for her, yearned for her, claiming her in every possible way, in the middle of his dreams. Each delightful vision spiraled quickly into a horrific nightmare, ending with her silent, permanent escape.

He couldn't help the rapid-fire movement of his fingers whipping strokes over his cellphone's keyboard one last time. He couldn't stop trying. She'd have to respond at some point. Right?

I miss you.

He just laid the phone on the cushion next to him when he decided to pick it up. There was one more thing he wanted to do. Pulling up his contacts, he pressed her name and then the call button. He listened as it connected and then counted each ring, his nerves on edge anticipating the sweet sound of her voice.

"Gabe... Please. Stop."

Grabbing, first, at the air, he snatched up the smooth rectangular edges of the phone as it threatened to spill out of his hands and make contact with the floor. A whooshing sound left his lungs when he tasted victory. He curled his fingers tighter around the contraption, squeezing its sides as if his life depended on his ability to hold on. He then drew in a deep breath of air before he spoke. "Listen, I know you're mad at me, but we can't go on like this. I miss you. You're my best friend. We always said we wouldn't let anything get between us."

"But, Gabe, this has. It's a big thing. I told you. I need time."

He snarled before he had the chance to check himself. Time. Time. How much more time did she need? He inhaled a second deep breath, attempting to defuse the tumultuous thunderstorm swirling through his gut, covering it up with peace and harmony instead. "How much time do you need?"

"I don't know. You threw a curveball at me."

He grumbled something unintelligible and shook his head. Why did he have to reveal his beast to her? He should've left the surprise for their wedding night. Nooo... That wasn't right either. Damn. There was no easy way of getting out of this.

"I know you must have questions for me. I'm here to answer them. Please, don't shut me out. Please, Arabelle, I love you. I'm not giving up."

He heard a long, breathy sigh. It was followed by a short pause. "I love you too, Gabe."

His heartbeats thundered through his sensitive eardrums. Competing, vibrant emotions swirled up through his gut, buzzed his heart back to life and landed, like a roadblock in his throat. He strove to regulate his sudden, erratic breaths and gasped out scant pops of air into the receiver.

Her voice lowered. "Gabe? Are you okay?"

He wanted to shout his response and announce to the entire world how happy she made him. Yet, his joyous reaction to her declaration might scare her. His brain stopped his mouth before his heart, impulsively, acted. "Yes. Yes, my love, I am." He paused several seconds to collect himself before he continued. "Please, come over. Let's talk and have a nice night together. Please. I miss you."

"I miss you, too, but...I don't know..." Her voice trailed off.

He couldn't lose her. He wouldn't lose her.

She interrupted his thoughts. Her cheery tone soothed his soul. "Thanks for the flowers you sent to me, by the way. They're beautiful. And the card... I love it."

"Let me pick you up then?" he offered, his heart filled with hope. He received her silence in return. He glanced at the screen as time passed just to make sure she didn't hang up on him. Afterward, he murmured her name in the form of a question.

"I don't know, Gabe. I don't think that's such a great idea...."

He closed his eyes. Things were fine before. He should never have revealed himself to her. The corners of his mouth slipped down with his disgruntled groan. Yet, his bear urged him to act.

To beg. Grovel. Roar. To do anything to win her back. Slamming through her front door and throwing her over his shoulder in a fireman's carry sounded pretty good at the moment. He'd make his way to his cabin and keep her there. Tied up, she'd never have the chance to run from him, ever again. He shook his head in protest while his bear groaned in misery at his current situation. He'd never keep her against her will. Besides, she'd hate it. He wanted her to come to him, freely, not as his prisoner.

Sometimes what his bear wanted didn't follow the rules of polite, human society. It wasn't that way in nature. What one wanted, one took, conquered, or died trying. Prey was stalked, subdued, and dominated. Granted, Arabelle wasn't prey. Yet, Gabe's beast definitely, wanted her.

"Meet me tomorrow then. At the pizzeria."

"I don't know…."

He begged her, uncaring how he came across. She was his mate, after all. He'd fight for her till the end. "Please, Belly, give me a chance. Please."

He sensed her hesitation in the short silence. "We'll see...."

He hurried to form a response. He had to end the call on a positive note. "I love you."

She whispered sweetly. "I love you too, Gabe."

"See you tomorrow." Quickly, he pressed the red button on the screen and smiled, ending the call before another word was exchanged. He laid his head back on his pillow, content to hold onto her final few words before he closed his eyes and surrendered to slumber.

She still loved him.

***

The next day proved long and grueling. After opening the pizza shop at ten a.m., each minute past that time, he spent watching the clock. Hopeful, at any second she'd show up, his heart skimmed through an array of vivid emotions. At the passing of each hour, he went through several stages. Agony preceded utter disappointment. Pathetic self-loathing soon followed. The final stage ended with intense bursts of anger. It was, currently, past one p.m., and there'd been no sign of her.

Each time the small bell hanging from the front door chimed, announcing a customer, he jerked his head toward it. He ended his perusals with a loud grunt of disapproval. Swinging his head back to the kitchen counter in front of him, he glanced to his right at his phone and then picked it up. Scanning the screen, he found nothing of interest. Arabelle hadn't bothered to call or text him yet. He dropped the phone back onto the counter, making sure the screen was facing up, just in case she contacted him.

Where was she, anyway? What was she doing? He pounded the pizza dough across the cutting board in front of him, unusually hard with the palm of his hands. Then, he added his fists. Damn it. Where was she? Why was she not here? Was it really that bad, his being a bear shifter? That he was unlike other humans? He never thought so. He never received complaints from past girlfriends. Besides, Arabelle knew who he really was. The only thing that changed was that he confessed his other side to her. Why was she punishing him for telling her the truth?

The fact that he was unique gave him extra strength and abilities human males didn't possess. Girls loved it when he tossed them into the air, no matter what their size. They got a thrill out of it. Some of the curvier ones he'd been with requested it, happy to have him parade them through rooms of their house or even into a hotel room. He carried them in his arms as if they were weightless because, to him, they practically were. His beast was able to lift and carry quite a load of weight. A mere two hundred pounds of curvaceous female was nothing within his capable hands.

Yet, here was the only woman he ever wanted- hesitant to be with him. A guttural groan slipped from his throat. He swiveled his head to find two cooks staring at him with a mixture of bewilderment and confusion written across their irises.

"You okay, boss?" The one named Paul asked.

"Yeah. I'll be fine." He never brought his personal life into his business. Ever. The only one who proved an exception to his unspoken rule was Arabelle. He shared everything with her. Yet, she wasn't a staff member. She now knew all about Gabe. There were no secrets now. He wanted none between them.

Paul piped up. "Hey. Where's your friend? What's her name, again? Ari something. Ara? Araba?"

He muttered her name through gritted teeth. "It's Arabelle." A streak of jealousy fueled his veins. Arabelle was his. They didn't need to know her name. She didn't visit his store for them.

His nostrils flared as he attempted to temper his growing frustration. His inhales and exhales were see-sawed as he envisioned smoke signals rising from the tip of his nose. Like a bull in Spain, he fancied himself within an arena of potential suitors. He stamped the ground with his hoofs and lowered his horns as he prepared to destroy the matador waving the red flag in front of his face. He drew in a deep breath as the vivid images disappeared. Although Paul was around the same age as Arabelle, he wasn't a potential suitor. Yet, the fact remained. He had *noticed* Arabelle.

Gabe had to remain cautious and vigilant. He never realized his co-workers took notice of his best friend. If he were honest with himself, he'd realize they'd be dumb not to. With generous curves in perfect proportion, a sweet kind, face, a matching stellar smile, and personality, Arabelle's very presence commanded attention. If she walked into a room full of people, they noticed. Gabe knew. He'd been witness to several unwanted voyeurs in the past.

Yet this didn't bother him. It was the fact that Paul brought her up and that she wasn't here in Gabe's pizza shop that disturbed him. Where in the hell was she, anyway? He sifted flour over the dough, pounded it till it knew who was master, and then rolled out the thick substance, once again to repeat the cycle.

"Hey boss, you didn't answer my question."

The dough, beneath his hands, suddenly morphed into Paul's face. The urge to grab the rolling pin and smash it to bits set his ragged nerves on edge and twitched every muscle within his arms. Keep it together, Gabe. Keep it together. He told himself until tonight. Tonight, he'd stalk her mercilessly. End up on her doorstep. Pound the shit out of her door until she opened it. And then? Then she'd get the spanking of her life. Hell. If she showed up today, he still might punish her in delicious ways for deserting him when he needed her, most. She deserved it. He needed her, always. She should've known that. Leaving him was not an option. Not without their mutual consent and agreement.

Gabe stared at the clock overhead until the big hand hit twelve. It was two p.m., and she was still not here. He sighed and turned his attention back to the dough. He left Paul's query hanging in the air. Let him, also, wonder where Arabelle went.

By three p.m., Gabe had enough. He was tired of staring at the front door, anticipating her entrance. Hope was lost. She wasn't going to appear. He'd spend the rest of the day behind closed doors lamenting his need to share with her his basic self.

Sauntering down the short hallway to his office, he shut the door behind him for some privacy. Leaning back on the door, briefly, he hung his head down and let the tears he withheld for the past few hours stream long, winding trails down his cheeks. He shoved his hands over his eyes and swiped at them in an attempt to disarm their rapid descent when several slipped past his fingers. He cursed and sniffed, inhaling a glob of snot with his attempt to regain his composure. He grimaced as he wiped the back of his hand beneath his nostrils. All sense of decorum was out the window. He could care less what he looked like. She wasn't going to show up.

He shoved the padded, executive-style chair behind him and took a seat. Rolling the chair toward his desk, he glanced at the screen of his laptop, unlocked the screensaver, and stared, blankly, at the icons across his desktop. The desire to do any work escaped him. Yet, he couldn't sit in front of the computer and pretend to care for the next several hours until closing. Everything seemed pointless; now that Arabelle made it clear, she wasn't a part of his life.

Lying back in the chair, he attempted

to calm his shallow breaths and his exaggerated heartbeats as panic struck him hard. He balled his hands into fists, then splayed his fingers out and balled them once again in an attempt at progressive relaxation. Repeating the gesture until his fingers ached, he, silently, begged her to come. Why didn't she show up? Why? He glanced at his phone. The urge to text a nasty or sarcastic comment caused him to grit his teeth and resist. No matter what, he had to control his temper. He wouldn't do anything irrational.

Images of her sweet smile and the delicate, soft shape of her facial features intruded. He groaned as pleasant images of them hugging, kissing, and, finally, making love floated through his mind. Slamming his right fist against the desktop in frustration, he then opened his eyes wide, stilled, and listened, intently to determine if any of his staff were alerted and were running down the hallway, concerned for his welfare. Emitting a long, low sigh, he lay back in the chair when none came to his aid. They must've known to leave him alone.

If anyone wandered into his office right now, he had no idea what he'd tell them. There was no sane excuse for the fist-sized hole he pounded into the wooden table. The evidence of his rage was plainly clear. He'd have to find a way to fix the damage or, maybe, buy a new desk. Regardless, she still remained incognito. He fisted his hands again before he knew what happened. Yet, this time his hands weren't empty.

Popping out of his chair, he threw his arm overhead and slammed it forward, launching the object in his hands toward the back wall. The clear, crystal etched photo memorabilia of him and Arabelle smashed against the wall and shattered. Tiny glass shards showered the wooden floor. He darted over to it, immediately realizing his mistake. An overwhelming sense of regret clouded over him when he found nothing left to salvage. Throwing his hands overhead, he gritted his teeth and uttered a silent scream. Why in the world had he destroyed the delicate souvenir she gave him several years ago? He treasured every gift she gave him until now.

He jerked his head up with the soft knocking sound. Damn. Who was it now?

"Come in," he shouted. Closing the gap between his legs, he squared his broad shoulders and stepped in front of the damage in a likely, futile attempt to bar the visitor's view of what occurred. If the visitor was Arabelle, he'd fall straight to his knees and beg her forgiveness. Destroying her precious memento was the last thing he ever wanted to do.

His heart thumped cautiously as he watched the door swing in. It stuttered when a familiar voice rang through his ears.

A tall, athletic build female rushed toward him with open arms. "Happy birthday!" He turned away at the pungent smell of alcohol, leaving his right cheek exposed to her sudden kiss. Gently, he shoved her aside as she thrust a small, wrapped package at him.

"Marnie? What are you doing here?"

She waved off his comment. "It's your birthday, silly."

"That's tomorrow."

She sidled up to him with a mischievous smile. "Oh? Well, I'll give you your gift a day early then. We can celebrate all night- long." Slipping one end of her sparkly jacket off, she wriggled her shoulders and let the other side fall. Then she winked at Gabe. The come hither look plastered across her face used to excite Gabe. Today, it annoyed him.

"We're not together anymore."

She sat, casually, off to one side of the sofa and patted the cushion next to her. "Come on, Gabe. Don't be like that. It's your birthday."

"I told you it's not!"

Marnie bent forward, giving him a tawdry view down her blouse. "Sweetie, I think you'll like the gift that I got you." As if she wasn't aware that her assets were on full display, she kept the pose and awaited his response.

Gabe turned away from the distasteful sight that used to give him lustful ideas. "What are you trying to do? Seduce me?"

Grabbing ahold of the hem of her knee-length skirt, she slipped one hand up her inner thigh. Skimming the fabric straight up her leg, she deliberately exposed the lace trim of her panty. "Duh."

CHAPTER 13

GABRIEL

Gabe had enough. He purposely strolled toward her to end her shenanigans. Planting his large hands atop her shoulders, words rolled off his tongue in a gruff tone. "I'm not into games, Marnie. It was fun while we were together, but I'm with Arabelle now. I'm sure you know this since you went camping with her recently."

He hissed as her right hand grabbed ahold of his crotch. Before he had the chance to shove her aside, she started stroking him through his cotton work pants. Her eyes widened as his body reacted.

He jerked away from her. "Damn it, Marnie."

She pointed at him and then gave him a saucy smile. "You still want me. Come here and let me finish you off, properly, lover." She lowered her back onto the sofa.

"No. Get up. Get out! I'm expecting Arabelle any minute now."

"Oh? Is she coming, too? It'll be fun. You can have both of us for the price of one." Marnie winked. She spread her thighs wider across the cushions and beckoned him. "Or you can have me, first, and her later. I won't tell." Placing her index finger across her mouth, she uttered a soft shh.

Gabe grimaced. He stalked toward her and yanked her off the couch to her protesting squeal. "I told you. I'm- not- with- you. Please leave. Now."

Gabe hissed as she scraped her index finger down his left cheek. "But lover..."

"You're drunk. Go home. I'll call you a ride."

She squared her shoulders back and huffed. Then she spat words at him. "I don't need a ride. I walked here just to get to you. And now you don't want me. Well, you know what you and Arabelle can do. You want that hussy? Well, you can have her." She swiveled on her heel when the door opened. Their eyes landed on the lovely intruder eying them.

Arabelle took several steps back. "Oh...am I interrupting something?"

Gabe's heart jolted. He lifted his arms out in front of him and rushed toward her. "No! Don't leave, please." He grabbed ahold of her arm. "You're here. I've been waiting all day for you."

Arabelle jutted her chin toward Marnie. "I can see that."

He shook his head seconds before he placed his hand behind Arabelle's back and led her inside the door frame. "She was just leaving." He held onto her. Reluctant to let her go, he was afraid she'd leave him the longer Marnie stayed.

He called to Marnie. "Marnie, go. You're not welcome here."

Marnie grabbed her shiny, thin jacket. She sneered at Gabe as she strolled by him, rolling her eyes at Arabelle before she slipped into the hallway. She gave them a backward middle finger wave. "You two deserve each other." Sashaying down the hallway, she exaggerated her hips as she walked away.

Gabe shrugged his shoulders at Arabelle's look of confusion, yet his hands kept ahold of her the entire time. She looked at the floor and then back up at him before wriggling out of his grip.

"What was that all about?"

Gabe pointed toward the wooden table next to the sofa. "She brought a gift for my birthday."

"But that's not till tomorrow."

"That's what I told her."

"Do you know what it is?"

"No."

"Why don't you open it?"

He shook his head. "I don't want to. Besides, it doesn't matter what she gave me. What matters is that you're here. I never thought you'd show up. I'm so glad you did." He smiled.

Arabelle's eyes searched the surrounding area. She gasped and then pointed toward a spot on the other side of the room. "What happened there? Did Marnie do that?"

Gabe's heart dropped into his stomach. He shook his head. "It was a lapse in judgment. I'm sorry, Arabelle. That was the glass memento you bought for me a while back. You know. The one from that picture we took, together, at the photo booth."

"Oh..." She slowly turned toward him. "I'm sorry I made you that mad."

"No. It's not your fault. I thought you'd never come back to me. I was angry. I should've known better."

"I'm really sorry, Gabe."

He opened his arms to her. "Come here. I really missed you."

She hesitated, at first, and then allowed his embrace. He squeezed her gently. Then, he laid his head on her shoulder and sighed with happiness. "My god, Arabelle. I missed you."

"I missed you too, Gabe. But I still

don't understand what Marnie was doing here. Does she want you back?"

He pulled out of the embrace. Brushing his hands down her shoulders, he gripped her arms and looked her in the eyes. "It doesn't matter. I don't want her. I want you. You hear me? Only you, Arabelle. It's always been only you."

She mashed her lips together as she considered Gabe's words.

He caressed the back of his fingers down her cheek. "Did you miss me, too?"

"Of course, I did. I love you. No…I'm in love with you, Gabe, but it's scary because now you are…you are…. "

He gave her a wide, toothy grin. "In love with you too."

The corners of her mouth curled up into a smile. A faint rose blush swept over her cheeks. There was something he had to do.

He swung away from her. Grabbing the wrapped gift off the side table, he tossed it into the garbage can next to his desk. He then returned to Arabelle's side. Sweeping his hands beneath hers, he held them in a light grip as he spoke. "I have no more secrets. I don't want anything else to come between us- ever. Are you okay with this?"

She glanced back at the ground and, slowly, nodded.

He tilted her chin up to meet his eyes.

"Are you free the rest of the night? How about tomorrow? I plan to take up your entire day. It's my birthday, after all."

She chuckled. "I'm still scared, Gabe. I love you so much. If anything happened...."

He silenced her with a sweet kiss that soon turned steamy. She grabbed ahold of patches of his hair, tugging gently at strands as he deepened the kiss. When he finally broke away, they were both left panting. He swallowed hard and then rubbed the tip of his nose to hers in a loving gesture. "Our love will get us through anything. I promise. You are my mate. I will not let you go."

She sighed into his arms. "I love you, Gabe. I really do. You make my heart happy."

He ran his fingers down her upper arms and caressed them. "And you make mine soar." He shifted her to the sofa. They sat side by side before she fell back into his arms. "Can I ask what made you change your mind?"

"I realized how silly I was. Yes, you're a bear shifter, but it doesn't really change who you, essentially, are. It only changes what you can do. I do have a question, though. If we have kids, will they be half-breeds? Is that the word for it? I guess part bear, part human?"

He tilted his head back and gave her

a boyish smile. "Are you telling me you want to have kids with me, Belly?"

She placed one hand on his chest and twisted her head up to look at him. "Wait a minute. Wait a doggone minute. I'm just asking questions here."

He chuckled at her antics. "Yes. I suppose they would be. It would be the first in my family. No matter what our kids end up being in the end, I will be proud to be their dad."

A wide grin plastered across her face. She closed her eyes and rested her head upon Gabe's chest. "That warms my heart to hear that. I think we'd have beautiful children."

He murmured softly by her ear seconds before he, playfully, nipped at her earlobe. "I think so, too."

She lifted up and gave him a peck on the nose. "I'm really sorry, Gabe. I never meant to hurt you. I was confused and- I didn't know what to do. I know I caused you pain, and I'm very sorry."

He planted a kiss across her lips. "That's okay. You're here now. That's all that matters. Besides, you can make it up to me tonight and all day tomorrow." He waggled his eyebrows to her girlish giggles. "Are you hungry, my love?"

"For your food? Always."

He, lovingly, nuzzled the back of her neck. His eager hands explored and caressed down the curves of her waist to the top of her round bottom. "We can have dessert later, but let me feed you first." He squeezed the top of each round globe before he lifted from the couch. With a quick kiss to her forehead, he swiveled away from her and stepped out into the hallway but not before he shook his index finger at her. "I'll be right back. Don't you dare go anywhere?"

She laughed. "No. You'll have to tell me to leave."

He winked. "Well then. You better get comfy on the sofa because that's never going to happen. I'll be right back." Shutting the door behind him, he strolled down the hallway to the grand kitchen, already preparing a shortlist of food and beverages he'd bring back with him.

CHAPTER 14

ARABELLE

When Arabelle strolled into Gabe's office, she almost walked out. Finding Gabe and Marnie together, after Marnie made it clear she was over him, had Arabelle second-guessing everything Marnie said to her on their camping trip. She considered Marnie a friend and, at times, a confidante. She made a mental note to re-think her friend's list and make necessary adjustments as soon as she got home.

She considered what might happen if she found Gabe and Marnie's heated bodies intimately entwined together and then thought better of it. Why was she torturing herself with images of Gabe with other women? He was only interested in her. That's what he said, to her, on more than one occasion. The fact that he was anything other than a human shouldn't deter from the fact that he tried to be honest with her at all times. Except for that one big secret he withheld from her the entire time they'd known each other. The reminder of the intense pain she suffered recently struck her hard in the gut. She chose to ignore it- for now.

He was still Gabe. He remained her best friend and the superb man she'd known since childhood. If he said she was the only one for him, she had to believe him. The idea that he craved, only her, made her over the top happy and filled her heart to the brim with pride. Gabe was a stellar, amazing catch for any female. The fact that he wanted her still had her insides swirling with glee. If this was all a dream, Arabelle never wanted to open her eyes.

After Gabe begged her to come by his workplace, she considered all the ways their reunion might go wrong. Then she considered all the ways it might go right. She decided to take a chance and show up despite her cautious brain warning her that her decision might prove to be the worst one she ever made. She loved Gabe. She had to strive to be there for him. Besides, tonight was New Year's Eve. She wanted to spend the ending of the year with the one she loved. That person was Gabe- her best friend in the entire world.

Walking through the front door of his pizzeria, she prepared for him to, suddenly, appear as soon as her feet stepped through the doorway. Yet, he was, strangely, nowhere in sight. The behavior was unusual for him as he always enjoyed being in the middle of the daily bustle and sometimes chaos of his restaurant. Being present and available to his guests and his staff was important to him. From his point of view, it was paramount to the success of a business. When Arabelle found Gabe missing, she knew something was up. Yet, Paul let her know he was in his office. He neglected to mention he wasn't alone.

Regardless of the previous, albeit disturbing events, Arabelle was happy to be with Gabe once again. Tonight, they'd watch the fireworks, or they'd make some of their own. Arabelle rubbed her thighs together with the heady anticipation of make-up sex with her sexy, growly bear. The idea of throwing herself atop Gabe and making love to him all night long had her mouth-watering and her panty soaked through. Forget the food. She was ready to partake in her delightful bear shifter.

Arabelle was consciously aware that tomorrow was Gabe's birthday. Still, unlike Marnie, she'd left his presents in her car, unsure if he wanted her to stay over or not. Although yesterday's conversation verified his enthusiasm for her and their continued relationship, today was another day. Arabelle never took anything for granted. Or at least she tried not to. People changed their minds all the time. Her past boyfriends did. In the end, she was happy none of them worked out, for she found someone a gazillion times better. And to think- he was in her life all along. He only had to notice her.

She lifted from the couch and scrambled to the door when it swished open. Reaching her arms out in front of her, she took several plates into her hands and juggled them across the floor to his long, wooden desk.

"My god Gabe, you brought me a feast," she exclaimed, her eyes widening at the delicacies scattered about their combined trays.

"Anything for you, my love. I brought you all your favorites."

She tilted her head to one side. "You know, you didn't have to do this."

He dropped the last tray next to hers and then surrounded her in his arms. Pulling her to his chest, he lowered his face near her shoulder and murmured, "I'll do anything for you. Anything."

She pulled back to look into his eyes. "I love you, Gabe, so much."

"And I love you." He reached into his pocket and brought out two wrapped packets of silverware. Handing one to her, he indicated the sofa. "Shall we?"

Grabbing ahold of both packets, she tossed the silverware next to the heaping trays of food and turned back to Gabe. "I'm hungry but not for food. I have something else in mind."

He raised an eyebrow. "Oh?"

She pulled him to the couch with a shy grin. "Is this okay?"

He softly chuckled. "Don't you know by now that anything you do with me is okay? Besides, it's New Year's. We can create our own fireworks. Just let me get the door first. I don't want anyone walking in or seeing your sexy, naked behind. That's meant for me." He winked before giving her a light tap on her bottom. Swiveling on his heel, he headed to the door. Flipping the deadbolt once, he turned the knob a few times before nodding in satisfaction and returning to her side. He scooted next to her on the sofa. His warm breath, hovering over her lips, caused all kinds of giddy, heady sensations to swirl up inside her.

His husky tone of voice melted her insides. "Now, where were we?"

She giggled in delight as she grabbed ahold of his shirt and launched herself over his thighs. Planting herself dangerously close to the lengthening prize hidden beneath the seat of his pants, she gazed at him with a saucy smile splayed across her lips and teased. "Right here, Gabe. Exactly where I want you."

His smile widened as he pulled up something wedged behind a nearby cushion and the back of the couch. He shoved the soft, red, and white-rimmed colored object in front of her. The single, golden bell on the tip jangled with his arm movement. "I saved this for you. Do you remember it?"

She gave him a shy, girlish smile. "How could I forget? You wore it almost every time we made love."

"That's because you like it. Here, you wear it this time."

She shook her head and then looked him straight in the eyes. "No, I prefer it on you. I want to hear you jingle when you come."

His chest rumbled dangerously low, and his eye color darkened. Lowering his eyes at half-mast, his lush, dark-colored eyelashes swept over irises filled with lust. Her eyes widened as he shoved the hat down, securing the white, fur-lined brim across his forehead. He gave little warning. Uttering only an unearthly growl, he flipped her at an inhuman speed atop her knees on the sofa cushions. She squealed in delight. Her screams of excitement soon turned into gasps for life-giving air as Gabe played with her nipples and then gently but thoroughly drove her to insanity. Working her clit like a master musician, he surged forward at the same time. Arabelle ignored the friction of the material on her knees as Gabe see-sawed into her. She concentrated on the softness of her lover's hands, grasping her upper arms. The rhythmic touch of his body against hers and the jangling of the gold bell of his hat. The rough but-oh so sexy-slapping of his balls against her ass was just the erotic combination needed to excite her. She soon found her bliss, shouting her joy for all to hear as the bell on his hat jingled faster.

***

Their lovemaking lasted into the early morning hours. Arabelle faintly recalled the last thing she remembered. A bunch of people on T.V. shouted "Happy New Year" before she was surrounded, once again, by the man she loved. The number of times they made love, and the varied positions excited her every time she thought of it. Gabe was creative, playful, and loving. He also wore the hat each time she requested it, which was about every position they experimented with.

One would've sworn he memorized the pages of the Kama Sutra. They must've tried each technique by now. Yet, Arabelle wasn't going to go there. She wasn't going to consider the amount of lovers Gabe had in the past and the things they did. The fact remained, they were all from his past, and she was his present in more ways than one. She giggled at her observation. All that was left to do was for her to slap a big red bow on her body. As of today, Gabe had her for Christmas, New Year's, and now his birthday. She was more than happy to fulfill his wet dreams and turn them into reality.

She twisted toward him in the bed, pulling up on the bedsheets as they wrapped tightly around her body. Her jaw, slightly, opened when she caught twin brown irises gazing straight at her.

Gabe rumbled a satisfied sigh. "Good morning, beautiful."

"Good morning yourself, birthday boy. How long have you been awake?"

He smiled. "Just enough to admire you without your notice."

She, playfully, tapped him across the shoulder. "Why you..." He grabbed her and pulled her into his arms before she could feign protest.

She caught his mischievous grin. "I

love you, Belly. Thank you for my birthday gifts."

"Why, you rascal. I'm glad you enjoyed them, or shall we say, you enjoyed me. You haven't opened your real gifts yet."

"Oh yes, I have." He waggled his eyebrows. "Many, many times as a matter of fact."

"You're such a cad, but I love you. So much."

He planted gentle, sweet kisses across her cheek and down the side of her neck.

He nuzzled her nose with his. "You know what would make me ultimately happy?"

"Another go in the sheets?"

He chuckled. "No. Not that. Yet." His tone of voice sobered. "Move in with me."

Her heart leapt into her throat. She blinked. One glance at his face told her he was dead serious. Moving in with Gabe meant she'd have to give up her apartment, part of her freedom, and her beloved keys. She'd have to mail those change of address cards so the bill collectors knew where she was. She'd have to tell everybody her new phone number was Gabe's... She'd...

"Get out of your head, Belly. Say yes to me." He gently nosed the side of her cheek. "It's my birthday, by the way. I want this. I want you. Don't you want us?"

"Of course, I do."

He pulled back and looked at her, a look of sweet anticipation washing across his face. "Then, you'll move in with me?"

She, briefly, lowered her eyes. "Yes."

He tilted her chin up to look at him. "I know you're scared. So am I. I've never made this commitment to anyone before. But you're different. We'll get through anything as long as we're together."

She made a small sigh. "You're right. I don't know why I hesitated. I love you, and we're together now. It's just that it's so perfect. I guess I'm still waiting for the other shoe to drop. I feel like I'm in eternal bliss with you, and it shouldn't be so."

"I know what you mean, but we're mates. Remember that. Nothing will go wrong. And if it does, we can handle it. Together. Okay?"

She nodded.

"I love you, Belly. Let's go get your things." He swiveled away from her with a gleeful smile.

She, quickly, reached out to him. "Right now? But it's your birthday."

"Oh, right." He pulled her to him. "Maybe one more gift before we go then." He tugged at the bed sheet covering her breasts, unwinding the obstructive material from his view. She caught his wide grin seconds before he adjusted her body and then lowered himself between her thighs.

~THE END~

ALSO, BY TK LAWYER

(THE GUARDIAN LEAGUE)

Jasper
Centurion
Apollo
Aeron
Orion

STAND-ALONE NOVELS

Angels and Diamonds
Shifter Shorts
Serenade
Crossroads
Her Other Guardian
Nightfall
Jingle Bear

ANTHOLOGIES

Love on the Edge of Danger:
A Pandemic Romance Collection

PASSIONATE * PLAYFUL * PARANORMAL

International Bestselling Author, Tamara K. Lawyer, writes under the pseudonym TK Lawyer and was born in Colon, Panama. She moved to the United States with her family to pursue her post-secondary education aspirations and found her love of writing shortly after.

She writes sexy, heartwarming, paranormal, and contemporary romances. Her books often toe the line, straying from traditional ideas to open reader's minds and hearts to unlimited possibilities.

When she isn't reading or writing, she is likely spending time with her husband/best friend or catering to their lovable American Foxhound, Misfit, who steals all the attention in their house.

CONNECT WITH TK

Newsletter
https://landing.mailerlite.com/webforms/la
nding/b9u7a8
Twitter
www.twitter.com/tklawyerauthor
Amazon
www.amazon.com/author/tklawyer
Facebook
www.facebook.com/tklawyerauthor
Website
https://tklawyerauthor.wordpress.com/

Milton Keynes UK
Ingram Content Group UK Ltd.
UKHW040637040923
428018UK00001B/23

9 798223 961086